CRIME CLASSICS

The Tyler Mystery

CRIME CLASSICS

FRANCIS DURBRIDGE PRESENTS

The Tyler Mystery

A PAUL TEMPLE STORY

FRANCIS DURBRIDGE

ABOUT THE AUTHOR

Francis Henry Durbridge (1912–1998) was an English playwright and author born in Hull. In 1938, he created the character Paul Temple for the BBC radio serial *Send for Paul Temple*. A crime novelist and detective, the gentlemanly Temple solved numerous crimes with the help of Steve Trent, a Fleet Street journalist who later became his wife. The character was so popular that it spawned a 64-part big-budget television series (1969–71), a number of comic strips, four feature films and various translations.

Durbridge went on to forge a successful career as a writer for the stage and screen. The last of his plays, *Sweet Revenge*, was written in 1991.

This edition published in the UK by Arcturus Publishing Limited
26/27 Bickels Yard, 151–153 Bermondsey Street, London SE1 3HA

This edition published in Australia and New Zealand by Hinkler Books Pty Ltd
45-55 Fairchild Street, Heatherton Victoria 3202 Australia

Design and layout copyright © 2011 Arcturus Publishing Limited
Text copyright © The Estate of Francis Durbridge 1957

Cover artwork by Duncan Smith
Typesetting by Couper Street Type Co.

AD001951EN

Printed in the UK

CHAPTER ONE

At about ten-thirty on a Thursday evening in early May a prowl car of the Oxford Constabulary was patrolling the Chipping Norton road a few miles outside the city. There had been complaints of wild driving on this fast section during the lurid period immediately after the closing of the pubs.

Sergeant Long turned his Austin a few hundred yards past the "Welsh Harp" and began to motor decorously back towards Oxford. Only a few weeks earlier the landlord of the "Welsh Harp" had been warned for serving customers after the prescribed hour. He had made sure of emptying his premises in good time that night. The parking space out in front was already empty, and through the uncurtained windows the two policemen could see the proprietor and his barmaid as they moved among the deserted tables collecting the empties.

"Not much doing tonight," Long remarked to the constable at his side.

"Pay day tomorrow," Benson answered briefly. He was a man of deep thoughts and few words; he spoke in a curiously oblique way which implied more than he actually said.

Three miles further on, a signpost with the words lay by swam up into the headlights. As they passed the bay at the side of the road Benson screwed up his eyes to note the number of the solitary saloon car parked there.

"4006 JDR."

He repeated the number aloud and switched on the light which illuminated his message pad.

"Same number, all right."

Long had already applied the brakes. Both men had memorised the number as belonging to one of the cars stolen in Oxford that evening. He put the Austin into reverse and with one arm laid along the back of Benson's seat, manœuvred the police car back into the lay-by. Before he had stopped with his bumpers almost touching those of the stolen car Benson was out on the roadway.

The now abandoned saloon was a black Jaguar Mark VII. It was complete and undamaged. Benson opened the door, felt for the light switch and turned on the side-lights. Immediately he did so the interior light came on. Benson sniffed. His sensitive non-smoker's nostrils had detected a whiff of woman's perfume. He noted the ignition key still in the slot, the neatly folded travelling rug that lay undisturbed on the seat beside the driver.

"What's up?" Long called from the police car. "No ignition key, I suppose."

"Key's there, all right."

To Benson's tidy mind something about the situation did not make sense. Cars were frequently 'borrowed' by young men who could find no other way of arranging an hour's privacy with their girl friends. But if that were the case it was unlikely that the rug would have preserved its immaculate neatness. And how had the pair gone home? Surely they would not drive out of Oxford for the mere pleasure of walking back again. There were no houses close by to which they could have gone. A thought struck Benson and he checked the petrol gauge. The tank was still half full.

For no particular reason he walked slowly round the Mark VII. It happened that at this moment a pair of sports cars came racing up the road at full-speed – an Austin-Healey pursued by a Triumph. For a few seconds their brilliant lights floodlit the rear of the Jaguar and in that time Benson's eye was caught by a minute triangle of green at the edge of the luggage compartment lid. It was dark again before he could grip the chromium handle and open the lid. Instantly an automatic light came on inside the compartment, and at the same time the scent of perfume became stronger. The light illuminated the body of a young woman lying huddled on the corrugated rubber flooring. She was dressed as if she had changed to go out for the evening – a green ballet length dress, small handbag, necklace and bracelet to match, court shoes. Round her neck was a colourful silk scarf picturing well-known views of Paris. Benson, though he had never been there, recognised the base of the Eiffel Tower, the pillars of the Madeleine and the façade of the Opera. This scarf, instead of being folded casually round the girl's throat, had been knotted with savage tightness at the back of her neck. One look at her face was enough to show Benson that she had been strangled.

Carefully he closed the lid of the boot and walked to Sergeant Long's window.

"You and I aren't going to get much sleep tonight, Sergeant."

Steve Temple stood in front of the fire-place in her new drawing-room and tried to see it with the eyes of someone coming in for the first time. Did it look too much of a mixture? She and Paul had tried very hard to avoid the impersonal effect of a room which had been "done" by one of the fashionable interior decorators. Since it was they themselves who were going to live in the flat they had decided to decorate and furnish it according to their own personal tastes. If George II had to rub shoulders with Louis XIV, then that was just too bad.

It was barely a week since the Temples had moved into the Eaton Square flat. For months before that they had been brooding over wallpapers and pastel shades, selecting carpets and the additional pieces of furniture needed for the more spacious rooms of their new residence. Yet when the carpets had been laid and each article had been moved into is predestined position everything seemed just a little uneasy. Gradually, during the past week, the correct place for every chair, table or cabinet had revealed itself to them. The flat was at last beginning to look like a home, but the result was that both Temple and Steve had itching fingers. They could not leave things alone. Now, before she could check herself, Steve moved impulsively to transfer a bowl of flowers from the top of a tallboy to a low occasional table.

She was studying the effect with her head on one side when Temple's key sounded in the door of the flat. She heard it open and then close again with the comforting thud of a mass of mahogany going into place in an eighteen-inch wall. Temple's footsteps crossed the parquet floor of the hall without pausing and she visualised him throwing his hat onto the hall table as he passed.

As soon as he entered the room she could tell by the expression on his face that the meeting with his agent had turned out successfully. But she knew him too well to expect him to burst out with the news immediately.

"Hello, Steve."

He stopped, smiling at her, thinking how well the setting suited her. She had been created to stand against an Adam fireplace under a high ceiling, surrounded by the most skilful achievements of craftsmanship. Almost immediately his eye moved to the Queen Anne card-table standing now between the two tall windows. Steve had moved it there since he had gone out that morning. She studied his face anxiously.

"How do you think it looks in that position?"

Temple came into the middle of the room, eyeing the table judiciously.

"That's the right spot for it. Now that it's there I can't imagine why we wanted to put it anywhere else."

"I keep moving things and then putting them back again. Paul, do you think there'll ever come a time when we can say it's done? Sometimes I wonder if we've got the fidgets about the flat."

Temple nodded towards the empty space above the fireplace.

"When we find the right picture for that spot we'll draw the deadline, shall we? Make a rule that we shan't move anything for a month."

"Good idea. Now then. What are you going to have to drink?"

Steve walked to the huge bow-fronted corner cupboard and opened it with a flourish. Inside a light went on and revealed two well-stocked shelves of bottles. Temple stopped with his lighter half-way to his cigarette.

"By Timothy! There's enough booze to sink a battle-ship."

"I stocked up this morning. We shall need all this sooner or later and it looks rather gay, doesn't it? Liqueurs, port and brandy on that shelf, bits and pieces for cocktails down here. What'll you have?"

"I'll have gin and Cinzano, with a strong dash of Angostura bitters."

While Steve was mixing the drinks, Temple glanced at the paper which Steve had thrown on the sofa. It was open at the page on which the Tyler murder was reported. She handed him his glass, chilled by a marble-sized lump of ice from the baby refrigerator built into the back of the cupboard. Temple met her eyes as he sipped it, toasting her silently.

"It's wonderful to be able to get back home so quickly. I was with Watson only a quarter of an hour ago. If we were still living at the old place I'd have probably lunched in town."

"How did you get on with Watson?"

Steve tried to make the question sound casual, though she knew that Temple was holding something up his sleeve.

"How would you like a trip to Paris?"

"Paul! Do you really mean that?"

"I do. I've sold the film rights on my last book to an American company. They want me to go over to Paris the week after next and meet one of their producers – a chap called Pasterwake."

"Darling, how marvellous! I shall be able to buy some new clothes. I haven't a stitch to my back."

Steve parked her drink down on the mantelpiece and put her arms round his neck.

"If you haven't a stitch to your back," Temple retorted, "why did you insist on a built-in hanging cupboard running the whole length of your bedroom wall?"

"Fashions change, darling. Hadn't you heard about Balmain's exciting New Line?"

"And hadn't you heard about the Chancellor of the Exchequer's boring old line?"

"We'll get around that. This man Pasterwake will be reeking with dollars. You can ask him to give you an advance on the film rights. What day shall we go? We'll fly, of course. Can we stay at the 'Pompadour' again? I love being near the Champs-Élysées."

As she talked Steve disengaged herself from Temple and with apparent casualness picked up the paper from the sofa, folded it and pushed it in amongst the other periodicals in the magazine rack. Temple watched her with amusement. He could see perfectly clearly what was going on in her mind.

"You needn't bother, Steve. I've seen it already."

"Seen what, darling—?"

"The report of the Tyler murder."

"The Tyler murder? What's that?"

Steve knew he had seen through her, but for the sake of appearances she kept up the deception a little longer.

He took the paper out of the rack, found the passage and read it aloud:

"Police are still baffled by the case which has already become known as the Tyler Mystery. Blonde, pretty Betty Tyler, aged 24, was found strangled in a stolen car on the outskirts of Oxford the night before last by a police patrol car. Betty worked at the Oxford salon of Mariano, fashionable Mayfair beauty culturist, whence she had recently been transferred from London—"

"That's the *Courier*," interrupted Steve. "Have you seen the *Echo*?"

"Not yet."

"Let me read it to you: 'Scotland Yard has been called in by the Chief Constable of Oxford. Interviewed today at the Yard, Sir Graham Forbes denied a report that approaches had been made to Paul Temple, the well-known novelist and criminologist. Knowledgeable observers, however, reaffirm that this case sets precisely the kind of problem in which Temple has so often assisted the police in the past'."

Temple's eyes were thoughtful for a moment. Then he knocked his drink back and carried the empty glass to the corner cupboard.

"That's just journalistic patter. I've no intention of becoming involved in the Tyler affair. We've enough on our hands as it is, Steve."

"That's exactly what I think. When I read about this, I felt certain that Sir Graham would ask your help."

"So you hid the paper. Did you honestly think I wouldn't notice?"

"Not really." Steve grimaced at him impishly. "But I don't want to miss out on that Paris trip."

"You won't. The Tyler case is not going to upset our plans."

"I wish I could feel certain about that." Steve's expression had become moody. She fiddled absentmindedly with the flowers she had arranged in the bowl. "I have the funniest feeling that it's going to upset our plans very much."

"You and your intuition! How often does it really mean anything?"

Steve straightened up with a frown of mock sternness.

"More often than you're prepared to admit, Mr. T."

The following Wednesday was the first day of summer; not the calendar summer, but the true summer, whose coming is like a thief in the night – no man can foretell it. Temple was glad that his business took him along New Bond Street. The thoroughfare was crisp and gay in the warm morning sunshine. The slow-moving cars sparkled and after a chilly spring every woman worth her salt had come forth in a new summer creation. Even Mayfair Man had reduced his habitual vigilance against the climate. Umbrellas had been left at home and though the bowler could not be discarded without affronting protocol, it was being carried in the hand rather than upon the head. Temple himself had greeted the coming of summer by purchasing half a dozen bow ties at Maddingly's and had changed into one at the shop.

He called at Justerini and Brooks and over a glass of Conquistador sherry discussed with his wine merchant the vintages which he was going to lay down at the Eaton Square flat. His way back to Berkeley Square, where he had parked the Frazer Nash, took him past Anderson's Art Gallery. His thoughts were on burgundy and château-bottled clarets and he was almost past the window when he stopped. His eye had been arrested by a splash of Mediterranean colour. He went back slowly and stood studying the picture in the window with half-closed eyes. Though it was the only painting in the window it was displayed rather artificially on an easel and the drapings behind it were distracting. Temple could not easily visualise it on his own drawing-room wall.

On an impulse he walked into the shop. The moment he crossed the threshold he entered a world of decorous coolness and silence. The light in here was subdued after the sunshine outside and his feet were cushioned by a thick carpet of a discreet buff shade. There were pictures every-where, mostly modern. His eye was attacked by stark Gauginesque jibes at the female form and vivid fantasias on oriental or hispanic landscapes.

"Good morning, sir."

The voice might have come from a radio set. It was musical and carefully modulated. Its tone managed to suggest that the speaker was prepared to proffer the courtesy title of Sir to his customers but they must not infer thereby that he was in any sense inferior to them socially. The voice had come from behind Temple. He turned round.

The young man was quite as tall as Temple and met his scrutiny unblinkingly. He wore a very well-tailored suit of dark grey flannel with a horizontal stripe which Temple found a shade too bold. His shirt was of cream silk and the cuffs emerged just the correct distance from his coat sleeve. When he put a hand up to brush back a straying curl from his brow a set of gold cuff-links was displayed, stamped with some unchallengeable crest.

"Can I show you something, sir?"

"Yes. I'm interested in that picture you have in the window."

"Oh yes? The Kappel study of Port Manech."

"I thought it might be a Raoul Dufy."

"It's very much the same style," the young man looked at Temple with a little more interest. "You like it?"

"That's rather hard to say. As a picture I like it very much, but I'm wondering how it will look on the wall of my drawing-room."

"That's easily settled." The salesman had evidently decided from the cut of Temple's jib that he was a customer and not merely a sightseer. "We can send it round and you can try it. If you don't like the picture you have only to notify us and it will be taken away again. No obligation to you at all."

Seeing that the suggestion did not please Temple as much as most customers, he added: "Alternatively I can have it hung in our display-room right away."

"I think that's a better idea."

The young man spoke the name Tripp on a register only a little above his speaking voice and an old character in a baize apron appeared from the back of the shop.

"Tripp, will you bring the Kappel that's in the window into the display-room. If you'll come this way, sir."

He led Temple to a three-sided space at the back of the shop. One wall consisted of a number of hinged panels so that the approximate colour of any room could be provided as a background to the picture displayed.

"What colour is your drawing-room, sir?"

"Well," Temple hesitated, "I suppose you'd call it duck-egg blue."

"Something like – that?"

"Near enough."

The young man offered Temple a cigarette while Tripp laboured by with the picture and hung it on the wall, slightly skew-whiff. Temple refused, but he noted that the cigarette-case was gold and the lighter with which the salesman lit his own Benson and Hedges belonged to the same set.

"I like it," Temple said as soon as he saw the picture on the wall. "I can see what's wrong now. It's the frame. It would clash with the furniture. Our stuff is mostly antique."

The other man's eyebrows rose just a fraction, but he gave no other sign of his opinion of people who mingled modern art with antique furniture. He was too good a salesman. Temple interpreted his expression correctly but ignored it.

"I'd prefer a slightly more ornate frame. And I think a little depth in the frame would give a more three-dimensional effect to the picture."

"Certainly we can change the frame, sir." The salesman nodded to the waiting Tripp and led Temple to another section of the shop. After some consideration he selected a grey frame flecked with gilt which gave the stippled effect he was after.

"It will take a day or two to make the frame, you understand, sir. May we send it to you?"

"If you would. What's the price of the picture, by the way?"

"Forty guineas, sir. We'll send you the account in due course – and the name and address?"

"Temple."

"Paul Temple?" The young man glanced quickly up from the pad on which he was writing.

"That's right," Temple answered with a smile. "The address is 127a, Eaton Square."

"127a, Eaton Square."

"You've no idea what day it will be coming?"

"I can't say exactly, Mr. Temple, but it should be early next week. Say Monday or Tuesday."

"The sooner the better."

The young man had produced his wallet. He selected a visiting card from one of the pockets and handed it to Temple.

"Just in case there's any query."

Temple glanced at the card. It bore the name Stephen Brooks, written clearly in a Sweet Roman Hand, which he took to be a reproduction of the young man's own calligraphy. He picked up his hat from the table.

"Thank you for your help, Mr. Brooks."

"Not at all, sir. I hope I may have the pleasure again some day."

Even at the time Temple was puzzled by the peculiar emphasis which he placed on these words.

Temple drove himself home, his thoughts so occupied with his purchase that he did not pay any particular attention to the black Humber parked a little way down the street from his own entrance. He let himself into the flat, but before he could burst into the drawing-room, Charlie, the Temples' cook, butler, handyman and watchdog, emerged from the door leading to his own quarters.

"Hold it, Mr. T."

Charlie's voice was hushed and conspiratorial. Temple tried to hide the annoyance he always felt when addressed by initial. The thirty-year-old Cockney was a faithful and irreplaceable servant but his familiarity sometimes bordered on insolence.

"What is it, Charlie?"

"I've a message for you. It's from Mrs. T."

"From Mrs. Temple? Has she gone out?"

"No. She's in there." Charlie ignored the reproof implied in Temple's correction and stabbed a finger towards the closed drawing-room door. "But Sir Graham Forbes and that Inspector Vosper are here. She told me to warn you so as you could start thinking up your defence."

Temple smiled to himself as he laid a hand on the door knob. There was no need for Steve to worry. He had a good idea what had brought Sir Graham to the flat but he was as determined as she was not to be diverted from that trip to Paris. The knob turned under his hand as someone opened the door from inside. It was Steve. During the moment while the door screened them she shook one finger at him in a gesture of warning.

"Ah, there you are at last, darling," she said loudly. "Look who's come to visit us."

Sir Graham was facing the wall at the far side of the room, scrutinising the picture hung there through a monocle which he used like a magnifying glass. Detective Inspector Vosper had declined to remove his overcoat. As Temple entered he rose to his feet and nodded but left all the talking to his superior.

"Temple," boomed Sir Graham in the vibrant voice which in days long past he had developed in the forecourt of Buckingham Palace. "Good to see you again. I was telling Steve: I like the way you've done this place up. It's honest. Reflects your personalities. None of this nonsense – the Louis XIV salon, the Marie Antoinette boudoir. What wonderfully proportioned rooms these old houses have! I was just trying to figure out this painting. Looks like one of those Venetian fellows. It's original, of course."

The picture that had attracted Forbes' attention was a modest canvas about eighteen inches by twelve. It represented a wild, prophetic head with flaming cheeks and turbulent red hair.

"As a matter of fact you've put your finger on the gem of the bunch. That's a Tiepolo. John the Baptist."

"Is it, indeed?" Sir Graham turned on his heel to quiz the picture again. "I thought he confined himself to painting ceilings. *Trompe l'oeil* and that sort of thing."

"By no means. He's not so well known for his portraits but there are plenty of them."

Temple tried to dismiss the subject by his casual tone. He caught Steve's eye.

"I was just telling Sir Graham about our plans to visit Paris, darling." Steve spoke pointedly and Temple spotted Vosper's sudden embarrassed glance at Sir Graham. "What'll you drink, Paul?"

"Same as usual; Steve has looked after you, Sir Graham – Inspector?"

The two men lifted their still well-filled glasses to show that Steve had not failed to offer them hospitality. With a twinkle in his eye Temple watched Sir Graham move round the back of the sofa until he occupied the commanding position in front of the fireplace. It was the stance he habitually took up when he was about to broach some difficult business.

Forbes was an old friend of the Temples. He was a splendid example of an Englishman who has been shaped by the successive processes of school, university, military service and public office. At the age of sixty he was as fully in possession of his faculties as ever and had behind him a lifetime of rich experience. He was still handsome enough to attract the glances of women and when men saw him they were reminded of the Older Man who figures in advertisements for gentlemen's clothing – broad shoulders, bristling grey moustache, bushy eyebrows and a certain aura of unshakable confidence and authority.

"Well, Sir Graham, what brings you here? Did you and Vosper forsake the Yard to admire our pictures?"

"Well," admitted Sir Graham, rocking his weight slightly to and fro and studying the liquid in his glass. "Not entirely, I must admit. Have you heard anything lately of a character called Harry Shelford?"

"Harry Shelford?"

Temple repeated the name thoughtfully as he accepted the cocktail glass Steve handed him. He remembered Harry Shelford distinctly. He was a likeable bad-lot who had been mixed up in a fraud case some four years earlier. Temple had become involved in the investigations and was partly responsible for his being sentenced to two years in gaol. On his release Harry Shelford's first action had been to call on Temple and ask him for the loan of four hundred pounds; he intended, he said, to give up crime, go back to his old job. His idea was to open up a chemist's business in South Africa. Temple was so surprised – and amused – by the request that he lent Harry the money. Twelve months later, to his astonishment, he received repayment in full.

"No, I haven't heard anything from him – or about him – for over a year now. Why are you interested in him?"

"So far as you know he hasn't returned to this country?"

Temple shook his head.

"If he had done so I'm sure he would have got in touch with me – if only for another loan!"

"Mmm."

Sir Graham glanced towards Vosper and finished his whisky. Steve moved forward to replenish it but he said: "No more for me, thank you, Steve," and held on to the empty glass.

"Do you know anything about this Tyler affair?"

Steve looked at him sharply and then turned to study Temple's expression as he answered.

"I've read the headlines," he said casually. "That's about all."

"It's an interesting problem," Sir Graham continued in his most beguiling tone. "Just your cup of tea, in fact."

"I don't want to get involved, Sir Graham. Steve and I are pretty busy at the moment. We've had quite a time settling into the flat and now there's this trip to Paris."

"Suppose Harry Shelford is mixed up in the case – would you change your mind?"

"What makes you think he is?" Temple put the question warily. He had a soft spot for Harry.

Sir Graham looked down at Vosper and nodded. The Inspector opened the notebook he had been holding ready in his hand and balanced it on his knee. He eyed Temple sternly and cleared his throat. Sir Graham sank back into a chair, and Steve, passing close behind Temple's back as he sat balanced on the arm of a couch, murmured: "Here we go again."

"Betty Tyler was an employee at the Mayfair *salon de coiffure*" – Vosper pronounced the word as in Saloon Bar and with evident distaste – "of a hairdresser of Spanish nationality who is known by the name of Mariano. I understand that he's quite the rage among the fashionable set now. This Tyler girl was extremely attractive and she became friendly with a Mr. George Westeral – in fact she was soon engaged to him."

"Westeral?" Temple cut in. "I seem to know that name."

"The Honourable George Westeral," Sir Graham confirmed and Temple nodded. Westeral was one of the most eligible bachelors in London – wealthy, intelligent and good-looking. Temple associated him with photographs in the *Tatler* of society people attending race meetings.

"That must have put a few debutantes' noses out of joint!"

"It did," Sir Graham chuckled. "But his family didn't raise any objections. You must have read about it in the papers. They made quite a story about the engagement. However, I mustn't poach on Vosper's preserves."

The Inspector took a moment to pick up the thread of his tale after this interruption. He shot Sir Graham a slightly petulant glance before continuing.

"Well, the engagement did not last long. It was broken off suddenly and no reason was given. Mister Westeral told reporters that he and the girl had simply failed to hit it off but there was a general feeling that more lay behind it than that. The girl was very upset about it. I questioned her employer – this Mariano fellow." Again Vosper's nose wrinkled slightly as he pronounced the foreign name. "She asked him if she could be transferred to the new branch he was opening in Oxford. Mariano agreed. He gave her a few days off to find digs and she began work again the following week."

Vosper licked a forefinger and turned over a page of his notebook. Steve, watching her husband's face, had noted the two horizontal lines which always appeared between his brows when his interest was captured by a problem.

"On Thursday of last week, Westeral travelled to Oxford for the purpose of seeing Betty Tyler. He took her out to lunch—"

"Early closing day in Oxford," Temple observed. Vosper looked up sharply, caught off balance for just a moment. Then he smiled, like a batsman who spots a googly and plays it back to the bowler.

"Not at Mister Mariano's. The girl was back at work the same afternoon. But that night she was found by a police patrol in an abandoned car on the outskirts of Oxford – the Chipping Norton road to be precise. The car was a Jaguar which had been reported missing by its owner, an Oxford accountant named Gerald Walters. He had been at a late business conference and came out to find the car gone."

"She had been strangled and her body placed in the capacious luggage boot," supplied Temple. "That much I do know."

"Yes. Strangled with her own scarf."

"That's established, is it?"

"Quite definitely. It was a silk scarf of French manufacture printed with pictures of well-known monuments in Paris."

"'Strangling were surer, but this is quainter'," quoted Temple.

"What's that?"

"Nothing. Go on with the story."

"Naturally we checked up on Westeral. He claimed he knew nothing about it. He returned to London on the 3.24 from Oxford and went straight to his club, where he stayed till late that evening." Vosper saw Temple's eye stray and knew that he was thinking in terms of Bradshaw. "It's all right, Mr. Temple, there is a 3.24 from Oxford. And several people saw Westeral on that train. We checked at his club too and he definitely stayed there till close on midnight. He's telling the truth all right."

"Did he tell you why he went to Oxford in the first place?"

"Yes. I asked him that. He admitted that he went with the intention of persuading the girl to patch things up with him. He also admitted that he failed to do so."

The telephone bell had been ringing in the hall for several minutes. Now Charlie put his head round the door and looked at Temple enquiringly.

"I'm out, Charlie. Ask them to leave a number and I'll call back later. Go on, Inspector, sorry about the interruption."

Sir Graham, who was almost as accurate as Steve in assessing Temple's reactions, thought to himself: "He's hooked all right."

"I made exhaustive enquiries in Oxford," Vosper went on. "My best informant by a long way was a girl called Jill Graves, who also worked at Mariano's salon in Oxford. The girl Tyler, she told me, seemed very depressed after her lunch date with Westeral. She also told me that during the afternoon she answered the telephone. The caller asked to speak to Betty Tyler and gave his name as Harry. She heard the girl arrange to meet this mysterious Harry that evening. Neither Jill Graves nor anyone else could throw any light on the identity of 'Harry'. So far as is known she had never received a telephone call from him before."

The introduction of the name 'Harry' was a cue for Vosper to pause and stare at Temple. Temple stared back. During the short silence they could all hear the clatter of knives and plates as Charlie laid the table for lunch in the adjoining dining-room. Steve began to hum gently. Only Temple realised the significance of the tune she had hit on: "I love Paris—" He gave her an appreciative smile and helped himself to a cigarette from the box on the coffee table.

"Why should you assume that this unknown Harry has anything to do with my old friend Shelford? It's a common enough name."

The question was directed at Sir Graham and it was he who answered.

"When Betty Tyler's digs in Oxford were searched a piece of paper was found in the handbag she had been carrying during the day – just a small piece of paper such as you might tear out of a pocket notebook. It had the name Harry Shelford on it and the numerals 930."

"I still don't believe that Harry would have anything to do with murder. He's a thorough-going rascal, we know that. But he's not a dangerous criminal. He is the last type to commit murder."

"I agree," Sir Graham said peaceably. "But obviously that is a line of investigation which we cannot afford to neglect. That brings me to the real reason for our visit."

He stood up and once again took over the centre of the hearth rug. Vosper snapped the band of his notebook and stowed it away in some secret part of his clothing.

"Harry Shelford has a sister – a married sister called Mrs. Draper – who runs an extremely popular hotel called 'The Dutch Treat' at Sonning."

"I've heard of it. The food is reputed to be really good."

"Now, what I came to ask you was this: would you drive down to Sonning, talk to Mrs. Draper, find out where her brother is exactly and what he's up to?"

"She'll talk to you," Vosper put in with sad conviction. "If I approached her it would have to be on an official basis. She might take offence and refuse to help me at all. At the best she would be unlikely to say anything which might be detrimental to her brother."

"She knows you helped Harry when he was released. It will seem natural for you to inquire how he's getting on." Sir Graham turned from Temple to Steve. She was watching the exchange with a mischievous smile on her dark, attractive face. "Surely you and your husband could drive down to Sonning for lunch one day, Steve. It would help us out."

Temple relaxed. For Steve's sake he had been prepared to refuse. Now that the question had been put to her direct he would take his cue from her answer. She looked quizzically up at Sir Graham.

"We're not doing anything special tomorrow, Paul. It would be rather fun to sample the cooking at 'The Dutch Treat' and see if it's as good as everyone makes out."

CHAPTER TWO

"What do you know about this Mariano, Steve?"

Temple called through into the bedroom from his dressing-room. He and Steve had been to the theatre and then dined with some friends in Soho. They had refused an invitation to go on to a night club. Temple did not want to blunt his wits or palate on the eve of the outing to Sonning.

"I've never been to him myself. I prefer to stick to my Doris. But I believe he's really brilliant. Several of my friends have started going to him lately. He must be making a packet out of it. He's opened several branches in provincial towns."

"What sort of person is he himself?"

"Definitely rather glamorous, darling."

"Amorous?"

"Gerlamorous," Steve sang. "It's not very polite to shout at ladies from other rooms."

Temple undid his tie and walked to the threshold between the two rooms. His own dressing-room was square, utilitarian and exclusively mahogany. It was rather like the captain's cabin in a small naval vessel. After its dark severity the bedroom made his senses reel. He had given Steve a free hand with it. The carpet was a deep wine colour and all the furniture was white. Over the bed was suspended a kind of panoply, bordered with stiff nylon frills. Temple always felt a little like Don Juan when he invaded this essentially feminine domain.

Steve was sitting before her triple mirrors, sheathed in silk, combing her hair.

"In what way glamorous?" Temple asked suspiciously.

Steve stopped combing and gazed at her reflection.

"Well, he's handsome – and foreign, of course. Rather an actor, by all I can gather. I mean, he knows how to put himself across."

"Put himself across?"

"Yes, darling. Hairdressing is an art – at least ladies' hairdressing is. Mariano acts the part of an artist. But he's a very shrewd business man at the same time."

"How long has he been operating this racket?"

"I don't know exactly. He's only been fashionable since the war, but Mrs. Tenby-Whiteside was boasting to me the other day that she patronised him over twenty years ago. So he must have come to England in the early 'thirties some time."

"Not very shrewd of Mrs. T-W."

"What wasn't?"

"Giving her age away like that."

"We all give away something sometimes, darling," Steve said.

*

The silence which the Temples normally observed until they had finished breakfast was broken the following morning when Temple put the paper down beside his plate with an exclamation of annoyance.

"What's the matter, Paul?"

"These confounded gossip writers. If they can't mind their own business, they might at least try to get their facts right. The cheek of this: 'Sir Graham Forbes paid a flying visit to the new home of the Paul Temples in Eaton Square yesterday morning. The conversation turned on the Tyler mystery which has been causing heads to throb in Scotland Yard this past week. This confirms the rumour we reported the day before yesterday that Sir Graham had decided to consult Paul Temple on the Tyler case.'"

"They really are the limit."

Temple pushed his chair back.

"Aren't you going to have your second cup of coffee, darling?"

"Pour it out for me. I'll take it into the study. I have a lot of work to get through before we start for Sonning. You'll be ready at a quarter to twelve, won't you?"

Thanks to his dictaphone Temple managed to shift most of his correspondence before he was interrupted by Charlie rapping on his study door. By the clock on his desk – a birthday present from Steve – it was still only a quarter to eleven. Charlie was in shirt sleeves and braces, a garb strictly banned by Temple, and he was wearing a shabby apron.

"A gentleman to see you, Mr. Temple."

"Who is he?"

"Name of Books, Brooks or Broke – something like that."

"Where is he now?"

"I showed him into the drawing-room."

"Did you answer the door like that?"

"Well, I have to do housemaid's work, see, so naturally I dress like a housemaid."

"Since when have housemaids taken to wearing braces?"

Charlie was still trying to think up some unprintable reply when Temple closed the door of the drawing-room behind him. He had been puzzled for a moment by the name but as soon as he saw his visitor he connected it with the young man who had sold him the picture the previous day.

He was standing in the middle of the room with a large rectangular parcel balanced against his right hip. Temple greeted him and nodded towards the parcel.

"Don't tell me you've brought my picture already."

Brooks smiled rather self-consciously.

"We managed to push it through more quickly than I anticipated. Shall I unwrap it for you?"

"Yes, please do. I'll ring for someone to take the mess away."

Brooks produced a manicure set from his pocket and snipped the string with the scissors. Meanwhile Temple had been clearing the oddments from the mantelpiece. He turned his back on Brooks as the wrapping paper rustled.

"Would you mind putting it on the mantelpiece for me? Then I can get a proper first impression."

"Not at all." Temple heard Brooks cross the room and place the picture in its place.

"There we are."

Charlie entered the room and found Temple in the act of turning. His eyes went past his master to the object on the mantelpiece, and he uttered a simple word:

"Cor."

"Ah, that's better," Temple exclaimed. "I really do like it now. What do you think?"

Brooks pursed his lips, studying the picture as if he'd never seen it before.

"Yes, I must admit I do. When you said you were going to hang it among antiques I wondered. But it doesn't really clash."

"Why should it? Charlie, cart that paper away and ask Mrs. Temple if she'd join us."

Rattling the paper as loudly as he could to illustrate his disapproval of Temple's purchase, Charlie made a slow exit.

Steve was as delighted with the picture as Temple, but that did not prevent her from paying more than usual attention to Brooks. He had seemed to come to life on Steve's arrival as if he had suddenly found a friend in a foreign country. It was obvious that he was at his best with women – preferably young and attractive ones – and equally obvious that they were attracted by him.

"Haven't you offered Mr. Brooks a drink, darling?"

The reproof in Steve's voice was evident, but Brooks was already holding up his hand.

"It's a little too early for me, if you don't mind. Besides, I must be getting back to the shop."

Temple was ready to move towards the door but Brooks seemed to be searching for some excuse to stay a little longer. There was that awkward pause which host and hostess feel offers guests a good opportunity to take their leave and which they so often fail to take.

"I wonder if it would interest you," Brooks said hesitatingly – "there's an exhibition of Kappel's work on in Paris at the moment. I read in the paper that you were going there next week."

"That's right," Temple nodded. "We must try and get to see it."

To his annoyance, Steve made a remark which threatened to start the conversation off on a new tack.

"Do you know Paris well, Mr. Brooks?"

"Yes, I do. I have to go there quite a lot in connection with pictures we buy and sell. As a matter of fact my brother lives there. He's at the British Embassy. I was wondering—" Brooks' face had gone a little redder and he was registering almost boyish embarrassment. "I was wondering if I could ask a favour of you. You see, my brother's birthday is just two days after you arrive in Paris. Would you think it awful cheek if I asked you to take over a present I've bought for him? It's a box of some special Havana cigars which he can only get here in London. There won't be any duty to pay because I'll open the box and take one out."

Temple was surprised at this request from a comparative stranger, but Steve seemed to find it quite natural.

"We can do that, can't we, Paul?"

"Yes, of course, though in fact the customs – "

"That's very kind of you. I'll drop them in a day or two before you leave. I only wish I could take them myself. Paris is marvellous at this time of year. Do you stay anywhere special?"

"We usually go to the Hotel Pompadour," said Steve.

"The Pompadour? Then you'll be quite close to the Kappel exhibition; it's in the Rue Royale."

Temple at last managed to shepherd the talkative Brooks out of the flat. He went back to the drawing-room to find Steve at the window, waiting to watch their visitor as he went along the street.

"Something peculiar about that chap. You and he seemed to be getting on like a house on fire."

"Does that make him peculiar? I liked him but I felt that we weren't seeing the real person. All that surface charm seemed switched on for your benefit."

"For my benefit? Come on, Steve, you under-rate yourself. Now, we'll have to get a move on if we're to be at Sonning in time. We'll hang that picture when we get home this evening."

They were lucky with traffic and it was still only half-past twelve when the two-seater Frazer Nash passed the 30 limit sign on the far side of Maidenhead and Temple brought the speedometer needle up to 80, an easy cruising speed for the car.

"I'm going to be ready for this lunch," Steve said, looking up at the blue sky. "I wonder if we can eat outside."

The fine weather had continued and the trees lining the side of the road were a fresh, rich green. The hum of the tyres and the gentle swish of wind over the streamlined body were not enough to prevent conversation.

"I wonder if you'll get anything of interest out of Mrs. Draper."

"I don't expect to," Temple answered, his eye on the driving mirror. "I'm convinced that Harry Shelford had nothing to do with the Tyler business. I'm only doing this to make Sir Graham happy."

"Don't you think that the coincidence of this mysterious Harry who telephoned and Harry Shelford's name on the paper found in Betty Tyler's handbag is too strong to be – well, just coincidence?"

"Coincidences happen in everyday life which no one

would accept in fiction. What does this ass think he's trying to do?"

A white sports car Triumph had been catching up on the Frazer Nash for some miles and was now sitting on their tail about a hundred yards behind. Temple had waved the driver on but he had taken no notice. He was alone in the car and had lowered the windscreen flat onto the bonnet. His cap was pulled down over his face and he wore a fearsome pair of goggles. Temple was used to being challenged to a race by foolhardy owners of sports cars but he invariably declined, though he knew that the Frazer Nash was capable of showing a clean pair of heels to most of them.

He slowed to about sixty and at last the Triumph accelerated and went past them with a vulgar blare from its exhaust. The driver did not even glance at them. He then played that most infuriating of tricks: began to motor at a speed just slower than Temple's usual gait. The noise of his exhaust drowned conversation. Temple made up his mind to give the Frazer Nash the gun and leave the Triumph behind.

The road ahead was a fast straight stretch divided into three lanes. About four hundred yards away a car was stopped on the left-hand side. A little beyond it, coming towards them, was a massive Marston Valley brick lorry. Temple decided to bide his time, but at that moment the driver of the Triumph put out a gloved hand and gave the slowing down signal. Just as he came up to the parked car he waved the Frazer Nash on. Temple assumed that he intended to brake sharply and pull in behind the stationary car. The brick lorry was just coming level with it, but the centre lane was clear.

The Frazer Nash surged quickly from forty to sixty miles an hour as Temple pulled out to pass. It occurred to him that the Triumph was going to have to brake very sharply to avoid hitting the stationary car. Just at the last moment the goggled driver put his hand out and edged the Triumph on to the centre lane. Temple found himself being forced out towards the oncoming bonnet of the brick lorry, now only thirty yards distant, his only way through blocked.

There was no time to sound a horn or curse. The lesser of two evils was to shunt the Triumph but even that would mean an impact of fifty miles an hour and Steve's forehead was terribly close to the dashboard.

The man at the wheel of the brick lorry, with the vigilance typical of British transport drivers, applied his vacuum brakes and stopped the vehicle in its own length. Temple swerved sharply to the right, aiming the Frazer Nash across the front of the brick lorry. Nothing but a machine developed in trials and racing would have accepted the brutal change of direction; tyres shrieked but the car remained on four wheels. She missed the lorry by two feet, rushed on to the grass verge and passed between two trees.

Still miraculously in control, Temple put her through an open gate into a grass field beyond. The car skidded on the soft surface and ended up facing the gate through which it had come. Temple had kept his engine running. He selected bottom gear and drove back on to the grass verge.

"Sorry, Steve. It was the only way out."

Steve produced a compact and began to powder her nose with slightly trembling hands. Temple switched off his engine and took a deep breath before he stepped out of the car. The lorry driver had driven another hundred yards up the road and was climbing down from his cab. The white Triumph, now moving very fast, was just disappearing round a distant bend.

Temple went to meet the lorry driver as he walked towards them.

"Your missus all right, mate?"

"Yes, thanks. I'd like to thank you for keeping your brakes in good order and using them so promptly. It saved our lives."

The driver scratched the back of his head and stared down the road.

"Didn't even stop, the— . Pity we couldn't get his number."

Temple offered his cigarette-case to the driver without answering. He had made a mental note of the Triumph's registration number when it first passed him.

He intended to write it down in his diary before he rejoined Steve.

"Police ought to do something about them sort of drivers," the lorry man went on. "If he'd been trying to do it deliberate he couldn't have put you in a worse spot."

Out of respect for Steve's nerves, Temple drove slowly the rest of the way to Sonning. Neither of them spoke a word until they had turned off the main road and were idling down the minor road that led to the village. Then Steve turned to examine Temple's profile.

"Paul. That was a deliberate attempt to kill us."

Temple was ready for the remark. He took his eye off the road for long enough to give Steve a reassuring smile.

"I don't think so, Steve. Probably some idiot who doesn't know his car. Too many of these fast machines get into the hands of people who can't control them."

"I thought he controlled his rather skilfully," Steve remarked drily. "His timing was absolutely perfect."

"The Dutch Treat" stood on the river bank just beyond the Sonning bridge. On a well kept lawn between the verandah and the water were placed a number of gaily painted tables and chairs, shaded by striped Continental style sun-shades tipped at rakish angles. Temple parked the car, then Steve and he went into the building by the hotel entrance. Steve said she wanted to fix her hair, and while she went off to the Ladies' Room Temple waited in the foyer.

He caught the eye of the reception clerk and went over to speak to him.

"Mrs. Draper owns this place now, doesn't she?"

"That is so, sir."

The clerk, hardly glancing at him, answered in the impersonal manner of his kind.

"Can you tell me where I would find her?"

"Perhaps I can help you, sir?"

"I'm afraid not. This is a personal matter."

"Mrs. Draper is not in the hotel, sir. She will not be returning till after lunch."

"Well, we are lunching here, so it doesn't matter very much. When she returns will you tell her that Mr. Temple would like to have a word with her?"

"Very good, sir."

Temple was amused to note that as he turned away the clerk returned not to his register of guests but to study a copy of the *Sporting Life*. The reference book which he pulled down from a shelf was not a Bradshaw but Ruff's *Guide to the Turf*.

There was still no sign of Steve. Temple noticed a public call box at the end of the foyer. It was unoccupied. He went over to it slowly, closed the door on himself and asked for Vosper's number at Scotland Yard. The Inspector had gone home to lunch, but his assistant was there.

Temple gave him the number of the offending Triumph and suggested he should check up on it. He was about to open the door and step out, when he hesitated. A man, emerging from the passage which led to the dining room, had entered the foyer at the same moment as Steve reappeared. He was only a few yards from Temple's call box. When he looked towards Steve he stopped dead, and a flicker of surprise crossed his face. He turned on his heel and went quickly back the way he had come. As he passed, Temple made a note of his features. He was aged about forty-seven or -eight, athletically built, though rather on the short side, clean shaven and well dressed in a tweedy kind of way. Steve had not noticed him and he had certainly not spotted Temple in the gloom of the call box.

Temple claimed Steve and together they went through to the dining room. For the summer season the dining room had been extended on to the verandah and boxes of flowers on stands lined the glass walls. The whole effect was very French. It remained to be seen, Temple thought, whether the cooking came up to the same standard.

A *maître d'hôtel*, poised before a desk bearing the list of table reservations, waylaid them as they entered.

"Name, sir?"

"Temple. I telephoned last night."

"Ah, Mr. Paul Temple, isn't it? I have a nice table for you, sir."

After an appreciative glance at Steve in her neat suit

and flame-coloured shirt and shoes, the *maître d'hôtel*, walking with unction and brandishing his pencil as if it were a conductor's baton, led them to a table flanked by tumbling geraniums. At a twitch of his fingers, a pair of waiters materialised from the carpet and set in front of Steve and Temple a couple of menus as big as railway posters.

When they had given their order Steve folded her hands and looked around her with appreciation.

"It's rather nice to be alive, isn't it? We so very nearly weren't. You can't fool me, you know. I saw you coming out of that call box."

Temple sipped his Tio Pepe and concentrated on Steve. A quick glance round the room had shown him that the startled man he had seen in the foyer was not here. Several faces had turned towards him with recognition, but there was no one he knew.

"Perhaps it did look rather like a deliberate attempt—"

"Looked like! If you hadn't spotted that gap in the wall we'd have been finished. Was it anyone you'd seen before?"

Temple shook his head.

"Even if it had been I wouldn't have recognised him with all that stuff on his face."

"But why pick on us?"

"The only reason I can think of is that someone is under the impression that I am investigating the Tyler case. Though why that should justify my execution I fail to see."

At that moment the service squad arrived with the eats and drinks for the Temple's first course. During the next hour they were far too preoccupied with the pleasures of living to worry about their escape from death. Mrs. Draper's imported chef was a genius and Temple rejoiced to have found for once an establishment which did not grudge the few shillings needed to supply the kitchen with adequate wine for the sauces.

After the meal, at the *maître d'hôtel's* suggestion, they took their coffee in a pleasant sun lounge built out over the water. They were still there, fingering liqueur glasses, when Mrs. Draper came up and introduced herself.

Lucille Draper was a striking woman. She looked a good deal less than her forty-odd years; only a certain severity of expression, reflected in the cut of her black suit, showed that she had seen some of the darker side of life. She had accepted her widowhood as a challenge and had put all the money left by her husband into "The Dutch Treat". She seemed to have an exceptional gift for business and in a very few years she had turned the hotel into one of the most popular out-of-town rendezvous.

She had heard a great deal about Temple from her brother and her pleasure at meeting him and Steve appeared quite genuine. She accepted Temple's invitation to join them for a few minutes, but refused a liqueur or coffee. She seemed to sense that there was more than affability in his request to speak to her. Temple was perfectly frank with her. After complimenting her on the cuisine and service he came to the point.

"What I really wanted to ask you, Mrs. Draper, was whether you could give me any news of Harry?"

Temple purposely kept his eyes on his liqueur glass as he asked the question. He knew he could rely on Steve to watch her reaction.

Mrs. Draper answered without the slightest hesitation: "It's funny you should ask me that. I had a letter from Harry only two days ago. He's doing wonderfully well out there."

She leaned towards Temple and gave him the full benefit of very blue eyes.

"I shall always be so grateful to you for helping Harry in the way you did. Giving him that money was the most generous—"

"I didn't give it to him," Temple said uncomfortably. "It was only a loan – which he repaid in full."

Lucille Draper, with a gesture which appeared sincere and impulsive, laid a hand on his arm. Her nails were deep scarlet and several diamonds glistened on her fingers.

"But it was the gesture that counted! He felt that someone really had faith in him."

Temple tried unsuccessfully to imagine the hard-bitten Harry Shelford voicing any such sentiment. He tried to steer the conversation back on to course.

"He wrote you from Cape Town?"

"Yes. Of course he travels a lot – searching out really good secondhand cars, you know. He takes care not to sell anything shoddy."

"Forgive my interrupting, Mrs. Draper. Has Harry ever talked of coming back to England?"

Mrs. Draper's pretty mouth remained open for a few moments to express her amazement. Then she gave a tinkle of laughter.

"That's the last thing he would do. Why should he come back to England when he's making a fortune out there? And an honest one, too. Harry's going straight now, Mr. Temple, I can assure you of that. He wouldn't let you down; not after what you did for him."

Just for a moment Temple believed he detected real sincerity in her voice. He did not try to question her any further. After a few moments of small talk during which she turned rather ostentatiously to Steve, as if inviting her to join a private conversation, she claimed pressure of business and rose.

When she had disappeared into the hotel proper, Temple turned to Steve with a smile. She was looking daggers.

"Well?"

"Bogus, from the peroxide down."

"I'm not worried about whether she bleaches her hair or not. Am I mistaken, or was she covering something up?"

Steve grinned at a private thought.

"I was watching her when you first asked her about Harry. She was ready for the question and waiting for it."

"I thought she was a shade too glib. Of course it's difficult not having met her before. Some women are always like that with men, but she seemed somehow strained, brittle—"

"I know what you mean. She's worried about something. Do you know why she refused coffee?"

"No."

"Because her hands weren't steady. And she didn't dare to look my way till the interrogation was over. She knew another woman would see through her."

The Temples were loth to leave the pleasant lazy atmosphere of Sonning on a warm May day. It was four thirty before they arrived back in Eaton Square.

Charlie had left a note propped on the hall table: "See me soon as you come in".

Steve picked it up and threw Temple a despairing look. Charlie answered the drawing-room bell promptly.

"There was a telephone call for you about an hour ago. From Guildford. It was a girl – she seemed young, anyway – called Jane Dallas. She wanted to speak to you personally. Sounded pretty desperate, she did."

"What did she want to speak to me about?"

"She wouldn't say. She closed up when I told her you weren't available."

"Jane Dallas. She didn't mind giving her name, then?"

"Well," Charlie's face was disfigured by a self-satisfied smirk. "She thought I was you, see? When I answered the phone I said 'Eaton double two, double four – who's calling please?' She says, very quick like, 'Oh, Mr. Temple, my name is Jane Dallas. I have some very urgent—' Then I thought I'd better stop her before she spilled the beans."

Charlie gave such a vivid imitation of Temple's voice and that of the unknown Jane Dallas that he and Steve had to smile.

"All right, Charlie. Thanks."

Temple frowned thoughtfully at Steve as the door closed on Charlie.

"Guildford? We don't know anyone called Jane Dallas."

"Perhaps it's someone else who wants you to take cigars to her brother in Paris," Steve suggested lightly.

"Then she's going to be unlucky. Now, I'd better telephone Sir Graham. He'll be disappointed that we've nothing more definite for him."

Temple sat down beside the telephone table. He was about to lift the receiver when the bell began to ring. He picked it up and repeated his number.

The operator said, "Go ahead, Guildford."

It was a girl's voice, faint and distorted by interference on the line, but unmistakably frightened.

"This is Temple speaking."

"Oh, Mr. Temple. I read in the papers that you are

investigating the Tyler mystery. I have some very important information. I've got to see you immediately."

Jane Dallas sounded a very excitable young lady. There was a touch of hysteria in her voice.

Temple said: "The papers are misinformed. It's not true that I'm investigating the Tyler mystery. Your proper course is to take this information to the police."

"I can't do that, Mr. Temple. I've got to see you. It's impossible to explain on the telephone. Oh, can't you understand?"

The voice was becoming more and more overwrought.

"I'm afraid I can't come down to Guildford, Miss Dallas—"

"You must," the girl insisted. Then as if she felt the old tag would clinch matters: "It's a matter of life and death. I'm at 17 Charlotte Street. I'll expect you at nine o'clock tonight."

Before Temple had time to object there came a click and the line was dead.

"That," he told Steve, "was Jane Dallas."

"So I guessed. I could hear most of it from here. She didn't sound to me as if she was putting on an act."

"You mean you think I should have agreed to see her? What are the police for if not to deal with cases like this?"

"She may have vital information and yet be frightened, for no valid and sensible reason, of going to the police. I felt rather sorry for her."

This time it was Temple himself who began to whistle: "I love Paris—". Steve remained serious.

"You say you're not investigating the Tyler mystery but this morning someone tried to kill us on the Bath Road."

Temple sat motionless for a moment, then slapped his knee and stood up.

"All right. This evening we'll call on Miss Jane Dallas of 17 Charlotte Street. I'll tell Charlie we want an early dinner."

CHAPTER THREE

A thunderstorm passed across the Southern Counties that evening, bringing darkness on a little earlier than usual. The rain, while it lasted, was very heavy. Temple was forced to slow down at several points outside Guildford where the water had collected in hollows in the road.

He drove directly to the Police Station and left Steve sitting in the car outside whilst he went to inquire the whereabouts of Charlotte Street. He was out within three minutes.

"I think we'll walk," he said, and opened the door on Steve's side for her. "The place is only ten minutes away and it's not nine yet. I don't want to attract attention by driving the car up to her door."

Guildford's steep, narrow main street was still glistening wet. The lights from those shops whose owners considered that their window display justified keeping the illuminations on till midnight sent squiggles of orange, red and green across the roadway. Temple felt Steve's arm pulling on his as they passed a window where some new silk materials were displayed, draped round bogusly bosomed dummies. A little later she did stop dead, her arm hooked firmly in his elbow.

"Paul, look!"

They were opposite a brand new shop on one of the most prominent street corners in Guildford. The window display was highly imaginative and for a moment Temple was at a loss to tell what kind of merchandise this establishment was offering. The theme of the display was Mediterranean travel and night life in the gayer Riviera resorts. There were travel posters from Spain, France, Italy, Portugal and Yugoslavia, photographs of the Casino at San Remo, the Negresco in Cannes, and some unidentified night-spot in Barcelona. In the middle of all this colour and gaiety was the marble bust of a very beautiful, very twentieth-century woman.

Temple followed Steve's eyes to the sign painted in flowing letters above the window. "Mariano. Coiffeur de Dames."

"He gets around," Temple murmured.

Steve was enthusiastic about Mariano's window display.

"It's rather dashing, don't you think, darling? Better than that dreadful wax image with some dead person's hair planted on it like a wig."

In fact, Temple noticed, most of the people who emerged now that the rain was over, paused to inspect the gay posters and photographs.

A few hundred yards later they turned into Charlotte Street and crossed over to be on the right side for the odd numbers. The houses here were strictly uniform – arched porches flanked by bow windows and separated from the pavement by sad little patches of downtrodden grass. There was a light on in the hall of number 17 and the black figures stood out clearly on the crescent-shaped glass above the doorway. Temple followed Steve up the three steps and pushed the bell.

The door was opened by a plump and elderly lady who wiped her hands on her apron as she answered Temple's inquiry. Her name, they learned later, was Mrs. Hobson.

"Is Miss Dallas in?"

"No."

"This is the house, isn't it?"

"Yes, but she's not in."

"Did she leave any message for me? My name's Temple."

"No. She said nothing to me."

Mrs. Hobson had begun to close the door. She regarded Temple and Steve with suspicion, as if they spelt trouble.

"That's odd," he persisted. "I had an appointment to meet her here at nine o'clock. Has she not been in this evening at all?"

The woman shrugged as if to imply that the movements of her lodgers were no concern of hers.

"She may have come in and gone out again while I was out feeding my budgies. As often as not she only comes back for long enough to change her shoes or dress before hurrying off to the pictures or the Palais."

"Are you sure she's not in her room now?"

"You seem very inclined to doubt my word—" Mrs. Hobson was working herself up into a huff over Temple's insistence.

He said politely: "I've come all the way from London to see her, so naturally I don't want to miss her."

"From London, are you? Well, I can always tell whether Jane is in or not by her wireless. It switches on from the door as you go in and she's never in that room without it's on. I don't complain because I think she feels the loneliness."

"Well, thank you very much, Mrs.—er?"

"Hobson's my name."

"Mrs. Hobson. Perhaps we can call back a little later?"

"Yes. I'll tell her as soon as she comes in."

Temple was just turning away to go down the steps when a thought struck him.

"By the way, Mrs. Hobson, where does Miss Dallas work?"

Being called by her name seemed to make all the difference to the landlady. A little primness crept into her pronunciation but she answered more readily.

"She's employed at one of those hairdressing saloons. It's a new place – I can't remember the name just at the moment."

"Is it Mariano's?"

"That's it. I knew it was some French name."

Steve and Temple walked slowly back towards the main

street, watching for any girl coming the opposite way who might be Jane Dallas.

"Is this coincidence again?" Steve asked, though she already knew the answer.

"It can't be. This girl mentioned the Tyler mystery on the telephone. Perhaps she too was transferred from the London branch and knew Betty Tyler when they were there together."

"But Betty Tyler was murdered after she left London."

"We don't know that this 'Harry' business didn't begin when she was still there. I have a feeling that Jane Dallas is going to help us quite a lot." He glanced at his watch. "Ten past nine. I wonder how long we should give it?"

"Another twenty minutes," Steve suggested. "Let's go into this hotel and have a drink. I'm rather cold after that drive."

Temple was very much on edge and hardly gave Steve time to enjoy her brandy. They were back at the door of number 17 before the clocks started striking the half-hour.

"She's not back yet," Mrs. Hobson assured them. "I left my kitchen door open so that I'd hear the front door and no one's come in."

"Mrs. Hobson, I wonder if you'd just try her room – in case her radio has gone wrong or something."

"Well—" Mrs. Hobson surveyed Steve doubtfully and then opened the door wider. "Since you've come all the way from London."

They stood in the narrow hall while Mrs. Hobson toiled up the worn green stair carpet to the first floor. The "Monarch of the Glen" stared aloofly over their heads and a faint odour of primeval cabbage leaked out from the kitchen. In a minute or two Mrs. Hobson came back down the stairs, walking sideways and holding on to the banisters.

"There's no answer," she said. "But it's a funny thing, her door's locked. She never locks it when she goes out—"

Temple was already moving towards the staircase.

"Will you show me where her room is, please?"

"Why!" Mrs. Hobson put out a podgy hand to restrain him. "I'll ask you to remember whose house you're in."

"This is urgent," Temple snapped. "That girl may be in danger. Now, which is her room?"

Before the expression in his eyes, Mrs. Hobson capitulated.

"It's the door facing you at the end of the passage."

Jane Dallas's door was indeed locked. Temple banged on it and called loudly. Inside there was complete silence. Behind him he could hear Steve talking soothingly to the landlady, who was horrified at the sight of a Man on her first floor landing. He stood back a few feet, raised his right leg and kicked his heel against the door just below the lock. With a splintering sound the door shuddered open. The room in front of him was in darkness. He could see his own shadow, stretched to a grotesque length in the rectangle of light cast by the lamp on the landing.

With his left hand he felt for the light switch and snapped it on. He heard Steve coming along the passage behind him. Over his shoulder he said:

"Don't come any further, Steve. Try and get Mrs. Hobson downstairs."

Steve had worked with Temple too often to ignore that tone of voice. Without question she turned away. Temple went into the room and with the toe of his foot pushed the door until it was almost shut. Then he stood his ground and devoted a couple of minutes to what the police call "giving your eyes a chance".

The room was a small bed-sitter. It was badly proportioned and too high for its size. The wallpaper and furnishings supplied by Mrs. Hobson were ugly and shabby but here and there a few defiant gestures showed where Jane Dallas had tried to create a gayer, more feminine atmosphere. A flower-patterned curtain hung across one corner, obscuring the wash-stand, there was a vase of daffodils on the mantelshelf and a framed colour photo of Capri above it. The divan bed was covered with a striped blanket of many colours which might have come from North Africa, Persia or Birmingham.

The room was scrupulously tidy. Temple guessed that Jane Dallas had not had time to change her dress that evening.

She lay sprawled across the divan bed as if she had been flung there by violent hands. Her face was turned upwards towards the light and it was not possible to tell now whether she had been plain or pretty. Without moving from where he stood Temple was able to recognise the handiwork of a strangler. Though it was practically un-creased he never doubted that the girl had been killed with the silk picture scarf which lay near her on the divan. It had fallen in such a way that he could pick out on its shiny surface the Place de la Concorde, a portion of the Palais de Chaillot and Notre Dame de Paris.

Behind him a voice, growing rapidly in volume, an-nounced: "And now, in answer to many requests, Al Jacobs will sing that popular number 'Lonely is the Night'." An unseen multitude applauded and the brass section of an orchestra went into the key of E minor.

Temple calculated that Jane Dallas's radio took just about two minutes to warm up. He hooked his toe round the door again to pull it open, and went downstairs to telephone the police.

"I wish to God we could get a drink," Sir Graham grum-bled, scowling round the dark empty lounge of the "Black Lion". Some time earlier the waiter had politely pointed out that unless they were residents they could not be served with alcoholic refreshment. As a great favour he had brought them luke-warm liquid in a coffee jug; it tasted as if it had been distilled from acorns. Their still half-full cups stood on the table round which Steve, Forbes and Temple were sitting on cold, slippery leather chairs.

"Well," Temple reminded him. "It's your people who enforce the laws."

"They'd better not try and turn me out," the older man said in his bass-drum voice. "As a bona fide traveller I'm entitled to call for glasses of water till the cows come home."

It had taken Sir Graham exactly one hour from Temple's phone call to pick up Vosper and bring him down to Guildford. The Inspector had joined the Guildford C.I.D. men at 17 Charlotte Street; Forbes and the Temples cast themselves upon the mercy of the "Black Lion". While they waited for Vosper to bring back the latest information Temple briefed Sir Graham about the visit to Sonning, Jane Dallas's telephone call and his macabre discovery at Charlotte Street.

"She was killed, of course, to prevent her giving you this information, whatever it was."

Sir Graham picked up his coffee cup, examined its contents and then decided against drinking any more. Temple did not feel that any comment was required from him.

"What I don't understand," Forbes went on, "is why this strangler should leave his visiting card each time."

"The picture scarf of Paris? It didn't really tell us any

more than we knew already. The link between Jane Dallas and Betty Tyler was established. We cannot assume, though, that Jane Dallas was killed because she knew something which pointed to the identity of the other girl's murderer. She may have been killed for the same reason as Betty Tyler."

"That reason being?"

"Sir Graham, when we know that we'll be within sight of our murderer."

When Vosper came bustling in it was clear that he had news. He selected a straight-backed chair and pulled it forward to join the little circle. He worked his mouth about for a moment as if evaluating his thirst and glanced uncomfortably at the lounge clock, now pointing to twenty to twelve.

"Well," Sir Graham grunted impatiently.

"A very clean job," Vosper commented. "Just like the Tyler case. No fingerprints, no skin in the nails, no blood, no suspicious characters. She'd been dead less than an hour when you found her, Mr. Temple. Strangled, of course."

"You're checking up on her movements during the day?"

"Yes, yes." Vosper answered Sir Graham's query rather impatiently. He drew breath and created a significant pause so as to focus the attention of his listeners. "We have got something, though. The girl, bless her heart, kept a little appointment book. We found it in a small drawer in her dressing table. She seems to have had plenty of dates with boy friends. The one for this evening was what interested me."

Steve and Temple exchanged glances. This was Vosper in his most typical form, almost boyish in his relish for veiled mystery.

"The appointment was for ten o'clock. No meeting place was mentioned. But the boy friend's name was Harry Shelford."

Steve was hiding her yawns behind a gloved hand as they went up the two flights of stairs that led to their first floor flat. Charlie had left the hall light burning. Temple let Steve pass behind him into the flat before withdrawing his bunch of keys from the lock. He closed the door and shot the heavy bolt. Steve had picked up a pale violet envelope propped against a flat parcel on the hall table.

"For you, Paul."

Temple had recognised the precise, upright handwriting on the envelope. The note was brief. It simply conveyed Stephen Brooks' thanks for delivering the cigars to his brother and gave him an address in Paris. The box of cigars was loosely wrapped in brown paper. Temple opened it and verified that the seals had been broken and that one cigar had been extracted.

"Mr. Brooks doesn't waste much time," Temple remarked, inspecting the handwriting with interest. "A fast worker in more ways than one, I should say. Though rather ignorant of the customs regulations."

The following day's papers were full of the Guildford murder. Temple glanced through the half-dozen he always had delivered to the flat. Almost all of them were hammering the coincidence that both murders had been committed with a Parisian picture scarf and that both girls were employees of the fashionable Mariano. Temple had asked Vosper to keep his name out of it and so far at any rate none of the reporters had got on to the story that it was he who found the body. It could only be a matter of time, Temple reflected. He regretted now having given Mrs. Hobson his name.

Before going to bed the previous night Steve had expressed her intention of sleeping late the next morning. She did not arrive for breakfast until Temple had finished his coffee and was sitting back, thoughtfully smoking a cigarette. Almost before she had sat down he was studying her critically.

"When did you last have your hair done, darling?"

Steve froze in the act of pouring out black coffee.

"Do I look as bad as all that?"

"You look charming. It's a straight question."

"Oh, some time last week."

Steve was wearing her hair in the current fashion. Since

it curled naturally she found this both convenient and economical.

"Don't you think it's time you had it done again?"

Steve stared at her husband in amazement. His usual line was to protest at the frequency with which she went rushing off to her hairdresser.

"I suppose this moment comes in every woman's life. When your husband stops trying to prevent you going to the hairdresser and starts suggesting that you should go more often."

"Some of these fashionable *coiffeurs* are very artistic, they tell me," Temple continued casually. "What was the name of that chap we were talking about the other day?"

Steve put the coffee pot down with a bump and heaved a sigh.

"The penny's dropped. Sorry, it's these late nights that blunt me. Mariano's Mayfair place, you mean?"

"You might pick up some gossip about Betty Tyler and Jane Dallas. I presume these hairdressing girls don't work in absolute silence."

Steve rolled her eyes heavenwards.

"I should say not. You men talk about your bush tele-graph – you ain't seen nuffink. This visit to Mariano's is business, not pleasure. Agree?"

"Yes."

"In that case you can pay for the hair-do. My budget is not calculated to embrace Mariano's."

"That's fair enough. What's more I'll take you out to lunch afterwards. Where would you like to go? The Sturgeon?"

Steve telephoned to fix her appointment and was disappointed when the telephonist told her that Mariano's Salon was completely booked up for that morning.

"I'm very sorry to disappoint you, Mrs. Temple. I could fix you in tomorrow afternoon – oh, just one moment, please."

The girl broke off. Steve supposed she had covered the mouthpiece with her hand. For half a minute she heard nothing but the humming of the line. Then the telephonist suddenly spoke again.

"Are you there, Madam? I've just had a cancellation. I can fit you in at eleven o'clock this morning. Would that suit?"

"That'll do very well."

"Eleven o'clock, then. Your stylist will be Miss Browning."

"Stylist!" thought Steve as she rang off. "We *are* coming up in the world."

Mariano's Salon in Mayfair knocked the Guildford branch into a cocked hat. The motif of the window display was bullfighting. Life sized matadors in skin tight costumes twirled scarlet capes at incredibly ferocious bulls whose stiletto sharp horns passed within inches of their bellies.

The entrance hall was decorated to give the suggestion of a Spanish *patio*, with balconied windows overlooking it. A fountain played in one corner and instead of the banal fitted carpet the flooring consisted of polished tiles.

Hardly daring to speak English, Steve gave her name to the receptionist and was relieved when she was answered in her own tongue. A tiny page in matador's costume led her up to Miss Browning's cubicle on the first floor. It was clear that Mariano was doing very good business. There was an air of bustle about the place and Steve recognised several of the leading members of London's social set. Though it was hard to imagine that this glorified boudoir could be associated with anything so sinister as murder, she still felt a little like a spy penetrating into enemy territory.

The Spanish atmosphere ended on the threshold of Miss Browning's well-equipped cubicle and she herself was uncompromisingly, if charmingly, Scottish. At first Steve thought she was reserved and shy but she soon decided that the girl's nerves were very jumpy. It was not altogether surprising if Mariano's young women were becoming frightened. Two of their number had already been brutally murdered.

There was little chance to make conversation until her hair had been washed. Then, sitting back with a towel round her shoulders, she tried to break through the girl's nervousness by asking her what films she had seen and whether she went to the theatre. Given her cue, she was glad to talk and Steve was soon, at her invitation, calling her Kay. She had only lately come to London, having been transferred from Mariano's Edinburgh branch and was still trying to make friends. It was easy to bring the conversation round to the two murders. Kay confessed that she was indeed frightened; she seemed to find it a relief to talk to someone sympathetic.

"The police were here again this morning, questioning all the girls about Jane Dallas. Mr. Mariano wasn't at all pleased. Some of the customers were kept waiting quite a time. Of course, I couldn't tell them much myself. She'd gone to Guildford before I came."

"Did you know Betty Tyler at all?"

Steve and Kay were carrying on that peculiarly indirect form of conversation when each person addresses the other's reflection in the mirror.

"I knew her to speak to, of course. She was a lovely girl. She was a real lady, if you know what I mean. More like one of the customers than one of us." Steve saw her smile to herself as if at a pleasant memory. "I was very upset when her engagement was broken off. They'd have made a lovely couple."

"I believe he's a very good-looking man."

"Oh, yes. And a real gentleman, too." Kay straightened up and her eyes took on a starry quality. "I remember one evening I was going out of the shop with Betty and this good-looking man was waiting outside – she hadn't been expecting him, you see. Well, when Betty introduced me he asked me to join them for dinner. I shall never forget it. We went in a taxi and had dinner at the Savoy Grill. It's the first time I've been to the Savoy and I don't suppose I'll ever go again."

She brought her thoughts back to her work with an effort, made a little hollow in the towel round Steve's shoulders and planted a handful of fine hairpins in it.

"I suppose Betty was very upset when it was all broken off."

"She was quite changed. That's why she asked to go to Oxford, you know. Couldn't bear to see the familiar places without him, I daresay. It's my opinion it was his family."

"They didn't approve?"

"Well," Kay admitted, "they were very nice to her on the surface. But some of these old families are terribly snobbish."

Once under the dryer it was impossible for Steve to commune with anyone but herself. It was a disappointment that her 'stylist' was a recent addition to Mariano's London staff. While her hair was being combed out she did not try to bring the conversation back to the murders. But even if she had not learned much she at least had the satisfaction of knowing that her time had not been wasted. Her hair had been done very expertly.

Steve glanced at the pay check with curiosity as she

went downstairs to the *patio*. Mariano's charge for a shampoo and set was a highly professional guinea. With her tongue in her cheek, Steve told the girl at the cash desk that she wished to open an account and filled the form in with her husband's name.

"You wish to put today's charge down on account, Madame?"

"Yes, please."

"Well, if you will just wait a moment—"

"That will be all right, Miss Grant. I myself will vouch for Mrs. Temple."

The voice was close to Steve's ear. The cash girl looked up with a start and Steve turned slowly. She knew at once that she could be confronting none other than the famous Mariano himself.

Mariano was one of those small men who although they have to look up at most people, yet continue to appear formidable. He was squat, but his fullness consisted of bone and muscle rather than fat. His face was sun-tanned and patterned by various sets of tiny wrinkles; they did not make him seem older, but added force of character to his features. He had resisted the temptation to make his own hair an advertisement for the firm. It was short and innocent of brilliantine. His fingers were long, prominently jointed and spatulate at the tips. He had a way of holding them clear of his body, as women do when their nail varnish is drying. The near black double-breasted suit was impeccable and his hard collar was of the fashionable wide-splayed shape. A triangle of snowy silk protruded from his handkerchief pocket, a black pearl rested in the folds of his grey silk tie and a huge scarlet carnation breathed perfume from his lapel.

He held Steve's eyes with his own in a way which made her conscious and confident of her own attractiveness. There was about his whole manner a suggestion of suppressed dynamism. She would not have been surprised if he had burst into a wild *flamenco*.

Instead he said: "I am Mariano."

"I see you know my name already." He bowed from the waist and for a mad moment she wondered if she should have extended her fingers for him to kiss.

"It is your first visit to us, Mrs. Temple. I am content to see that you are intending to return to us."

His glance flickered to the account form she had been filling in.

"I was afraid that your coming was an isolated occasion."

Steve picked up her gloves and handbag. She had sensed the suggestion in Mariano's words. She was wishing now that she had not filled in the form with Paul's name. It seemed so obvious that she had come at his instigation.

"It was very good of you to fit me in at such short notice."

"Ill the wind that blows nothing good," Mariano said. He turned to walk with her towards the exit. "This morning has been all disorganisation. As soon as we open the police are here. Many of my clients do not like to be kept waiting. They cancel their appointments. I wonder if they are coming back to me again. In Oxford and Guildford it is the same thing. My business is being spoiled."

He put a hand on her arm so that instead of going out she was obliged to face him.

"Two so young and pretty girls." There were genuine tears in Mariano's eyes. Steve found it hard to tell whether they were caused by the loss of his customers or the death of two of his 'stylists'. "In England such a crime will not go without punishment. And when a man like your husband interests himself—"

"The papers exaggerate his interest," Steve said. She pulled on her gloves briskly. "As a matter of fact we're leaving for Paris very shortly."

"You ask me to believe that to come here this morning was coincidence for you?"

"Did you give me an appointment simply so that you could tell me all this?"

Mariano's arms stiffened, but his face registered nothing but concern and penitence.

"I have no wish to offend you, *Señora*. But I am a very unhappy man. The Metropolitan Police are not very understanding of a foreigner. I wondered if I could talk to your husband about this affair. Would he consent to see me?"

"I can't say whether he would or not. If you really are anxious to talk to him you could telephone him."

Mariano stepped back and again bowed from the waist with as much reverence as if Steve had just conferred a knighthood on him.

"For that, *Señora*, I thank you."

As she escaped into the street Steve was breathless. Mariano's company was somehow enervating. She found herself walking with an added spring to her step and wondered whether it was after all such a very bad thing if a gentleman's manner suggested that he found a lady, even a married lady, highly desirable.

Temple was rather quiet when Steve joined him at the Sturgeon. She put it down to the fact that she had kept him waiting. As they sat on high stools at the crescent shaped cocktail bar she tried to make up for it by giving him a colourful description of Mariano and his salon.

"I'm afraid I didn't find out anything useful. I expect he purposely gave me a girl who hadn't been in the place long."

"Was that just a line he was shooting – about wanting to see me, I mean?"

"I don't think so. He was upset about something, I feel convinced. Should I have given him a little more encouragement?"

"No, I think you handled it very well."

"I felt much more as if he was handling me. It's easy to see why he's become so much the rage—"

Steve continued, as she thought, to be rather amusing at Mariano's expense, but Temple was unresponsive. At last she broke off.

"Paul, is something wrong? What's happened since I saw you last?"

Temple finished the remains of his Martini and felt in his jacket pocket.

"I'm afraid I have a disappointment for you, Steve. Just after you went out I had this telegram from Pasterwake."

"What does it say?"

"He's not going to Paris after all. Says he's coming to London at the end of the month and will see me then."

"Then our trip's off."

"I'm afraid so."

Steve stared wistfully across the room for a few seconds; then she brightened.

"That proves my intuition was right. I told you we couldn't avoid being caught up in the Tyler mystery."

CHAPTER FOUR

Detective Inspector Vosper was sick of the sight of his office in Scotland Yard. His spirit rebelled against the idea of eating a supper of sandwiches and beer off his desk. He picked up his telephone receiver and dialled the number of the Temples' flat. It was Steve herself who answered.

"Are you in to dinner this evening, Mrs. Temple?"

"Yes, we are."

"I wonder if you'd feel like feeding a poor policeman. I want to talk to your husband and if I could eat at the same time I'd be killing two birds with one stone."

"We'd be delighted, Inspector. We have dinner at eight. Can you manage that all right?"

"I shall be there."

The Vosper whom Charlie showed into the Temples' room later that evening was gaunter than ever. His clothes had the crumpled look of a man's who has not been to bed for thirty-six hours. In spite of his fatigue he was pleased with himself and neither Steve nor Temple found it hard to guess that he had some interesting discovery to announce.

"After the past twenty-four hours this is a haven of rest."

His glance rested gratefully on Steve, who was spruce and colourful in a green taffeta dress. He accepted a whisky and soda, drank half of it at a draught and smacked his lips.

"How are things going?" Temple inquired. "Do you see any daylight yet?"

"That car which you say forced you off the road yesterday. Did you or Mrs. Temple see the driver? Could you give a description of him?"

"I'm afraid not. He was muffled up to the gills and his eyes were obscured by a pair of hideous goggles. Why do you ask?"

"We checked up on the number. You'll be surprised when I tell you the name of the owner."

"Well, for goodness' sake tell us."

Vosper took another mouthful of his whisky and soda.

"It belongs to the Honourable George Westeral."

"Westeral?" Temple echoed. "What do you think of that, Steve?"

"I simply can't believe it. What did he have to say for himself, Inspector? Did he deny being in the car at the time?"

"I haven't questioned him yet. I want to keep this little card up my sleeve – it's about the only card I have at the moment. But we're going to keep a much closer watch on him from now on."

Charlie knocked on the door to tell them that dinner

was ready and Steve led the way through to the dining room.

"It's only a very simple meal, Inspector. Paul and I usually wait on ourselves when we're alone. Will you sit there?"

There was a hiatus in the conversation while everyone stood around the hot-plate where Charlie had left a selection of dishes. None of the three wanted to be sitting down while the rest stood. At last Steve gave in and let the two men wait on her.

When everyone's plate and glass was stocked, Temple prompted Vosper.

"It's a pretty sticky case, then?"

"We're getting nowhere fast. All the usual avenues of inquiry have led us to a brick wall. Every one of Mariano's employees has been questioned and there's not one of them can even hint at a reason why anyone should want those two girls dead. I saw the gentleman himself again today. Had the effrontery to tell me my investigations were bad for his business. Over-dressed little peacock. I'll give him business, before I'm finished."

"I had a look at the inside of Mariano's myself today, Inspector – at Paul's suggestion."

"Oh, you did, did you?"

The Inspector put his fork down and stared from one to the other with interest.

"I think the girls are pretty frightened. You see the only

connecting link between these two cases is that they both worked at Mariano's. Some of the others are beginning to wonder if it'll be their turn next."

"They've no need to worry," the Inspector said confidently. "I have men watching all Mister Mariano's branches. But you're wrong when you say he's the only connecting link. There's our friend Shelford. When we pick him up we'll learn something. It can only be a matter of time. His description has gone to all ports and police stations. We know he can't have skipped the country because the net was down before last night's crime."

"You say Shelford can't have skipped the country," Temple said. "You're confident he was here in the first place?"

"Well," Vosper hedged. "We do at least know that he left South Africa about nine months ago. Though I'm bound to admit there's no record of his entering this country."

Temple waited until a decent interval had passed before he spoke again.

"By the way, I may be hearing from your friend Mariano shortly. He's threatened to ring me up."

"Threatened?"

"Well, I don't mean that exactly. When Steve saw him today he seemed very anxious to consult me."

"Did he now?" The Inspector turned to Steve with interest. "What did you say to that, Mrs. Temple?"

"I didn't give him very much encouragement, I'm afraid."

"If he makes any further approaches, Mr. Temple, I'd be very grateful if you would encourage him. I know he wasn't being frank with me. I want to know what he's holding back. When is it you go to Paris, sir?"

"As a matter of fact our trip to Paris is off, Inspector."

"That's off, is it?" Vosper said thoughtfully. He glanced towards Steve and winked. "He'll be wondering what to do with his spare time, won't he, Mrs. Temple?"

"I shall be doing no such thing," Temple returned warmly. "I'm trying to make an honest living by writing books."

"Paul, you did say you weren't going to start writing anything new for a month," Steve put in. "I can't help feeling rather uncomfortable about Jane Dallas. She may have been killed because of what she was going to say to you. It makes the whole thing seem so personal – I think we ought to help Sir Graham and the Inspector all we can."

Temple pushed his chair back and walked round behind Vosper to douse the methylated burner under the Cona coffee machine. Vosper twisted round to cock an eye at him.

"What do you say, Mr. Temple? Can I tell Sir Graham we can count on your help?"

"In for a penny, in for a pound," Temple said and Vosper rubbed his hands together. Automatically, he began to reach in his coat pocket for his pipe, then checked himself.

"Do you mind a pipe, Mrs. Temple?"

"Not at all," Steve said courageously, though she had learned to fear the fumes which escaped from Vosper's pipe.

"Have a cigar, Inspector," Temple suggested. "I'm going to have one."

"No, thank you. I would another time, but I've got to be getting back to the Yard."

Steve, struck by a sudden thought, stopped with her spoon poised above her coffee cup.

"Paul, if you're not going to Paris you'll have to return those cigars to Mr. Brooks."

"The same thing had just occurred to me. I'll give him a ring in the morning and ask him to pick them up."

Vosper stopped puffing at his pipe and looked at them sharply through a haze of browny grey smog.

"What's all this?"

"You're not supposed to be listening, Inspector. Paul and I almost became accomplices in an illicit smuggling racket."

Temple spent the following morning at Scotland Yard going over reports on the investigations made so far by the police into the murders of Betty Tyler and Jane Dallas. They had done their work with their usual exhaustive thoroughness, but, as Vosper had said, every line of inquiry led to a dead end. It was as if someone had committed two motiveless murders for the mere pleasure of baffling the police. Apart from the fact that his name had been found amongst the papers of both the murdered girls there was nothing to associate Shelford with the crimes. Indeed, Scotland Yard were convinced that if he had succeeded in getting back into the country undetected, it had been under a completely new name and identity.

Temple emerged from the building with the conviction that if the mystery were solved it would not be by the routine police method of working outwards from the crimes themselves, but by an indirect and unconventional approach. He was forced to admit, though, that at the moment he could not see how such an approach might be made.

When he returned home he found Steve sitting at the desk in his study looking very business-like.

"I've tidied your desk for you," she announced with satisfaction. "It was in an awful muddle."

"Oh, Lord! Now I shan't be able to find anything for a week. How many times have I told you that my papers are not to be disturbed?"

"Paul, you can't expect Mrs. Bleek to do the dusting if there are papers everywhere. You'll find everything in its logical place."

Temple shook his head and sat down in the armchair which he had provided for his own visitors.

"Any messages?"

"I rang up Anderson's Galleries. Would you believe it? Stephen Brooks has had to be rushed off to hospital for an emergency operation."

"What's wrong with him – appendicitis?"

"She didn't say."

"Who didn't say?"

"The girl who answered the phone. Terribly county, she was. One of those well-bred, drawly voices which are doing you a great favour by talking to you at all."

Temple laughed. "Did you tell her about the cigars?"

"Darling, girls don't talk about cigars. I expressed our regrets and rang off. He can pick them up when he comes out if he really wants them."

"Curious how suddenly it takes people. He seemed quite fit when he was here the other day. No one else rang up?"

"Oh, yes, they did. Mariano wanted to speak to you personally. I said you'd ring back. He'll be at the shop until one and it's not quite that yet."

Temple pulled his chair forward till he could reach the instrument on his desk.

"You've got his number?"

"Yes. I jotted it down on this pad."

Steve reversed the message pad so that Temple could see it while he dialled the number. Mariano's telephone operator put him through straight away.

"Mr. Temple, it is very good of you to call. Your wife

has told you that I am most anxious to consult with you?"

"Yes, she told me about that."

"If you are free this evening I would be delighted if you could have dinner with me."

"I'm afraid I can't dine. Could we meet for a drink?"

"With pleasure. May I await you in the downstairs bar at the Ritz at, let us say, a quarter-past six?"

"Yes. That'll suit me very well."

"Six-fifteen at the Ritz," Temple repeated for Steve's benefit when he had rung off.

"Good. Am I coming too?"

"Indeed you're not."

"Oh, Paul!"

"You can stay at home and tidy my desk. We must think of dear Mrs. Bleek."

Mariano was already waiting when Temple walked down the stairs into the cocktail bar at exactly six-fifteen. He seemed to know Temple by sight and rose to meet him. He had procured a table where they could talk without being overheard. He greeted Temple effusively and was masterful in seeing that his choice of drink was brought with the minimum of delay.

Temple studied him with interest and was once again astonished at the type of man who appeals to some women. Mariano was not a man's man. It was easy to see why Vosper had not found him easy to handle. The faint scent of perfume which Mariano exuded would by itself have been enough to antagonize the Inspector. He had probably tried to browbeat the Spaniard and Mariano was not a man to be flurried. Temple, though a great believer in the reliability of first impressions, found him unusually difficult to weigh up.

Once they were served Mariano lost no time in coming to business.

"Mr. Temple, I know you are a busy man and I have no intention to waste your time. I will be very frank. I have been fortunate with my little business. It has made quite a lot of money for me. Now that I have expanded – opened several new branches – I hope that it will make much more. But just at the moment when I make the big gamble this tragedy happens. These two unfortunate girls being murdered like that – it is very bad for my business."

He leant forward, crossing his wrists on the table. His cuffs moved back, disclosing a good watch strap. The watch itself remained invisible on the inside of his wrist.

"I have a proposition to put to you. I wish to engage you to investigate for me these two crimes. I am prepared to pay a considerable sum – probably any reasonable sum which you care to name."

Mariano spoke the words with peculiar intentness. His eyes, though they remained fixed on Temple's, were as inscrutable as a poker player's. Temple fingered the stem of his glass and moved sideways to cross his legs.

"What's your object in making me this offer, Mr. Mariano?"

Mariano's fingers were clasped together even more tightly than before.

"If you undertake this investigation for me the matter will be in all the papers. People will realise that Mariano is shocked by the murder of two of his girls. They will know that these tragedies have nothing to do with me or my business. You agree, Mr. Temple? We can start to talk about terms?"

Temple shook his head and smiled.

"You must take what you read about me in the papers with a pinch of salt. I'm first and foremost a writer. If I do take part in investigations it's for purely personal reasons. Sir Graham Forbes and I are old friends. I'm not in any sense what you would call a private detective."

Mariano unclasped his hands and opened them in a Continental gesture of apology.

"Forgive me. It is sometimes difficult for a foreigner to understand your delicate English situations. I have not insulted you?"

"By no means. I'm not so easily offended as all that. What are you drinking?"

"No. You are my guest." Mariano snapped his fingers at a passing waiter. Temple, however, called him by name and had the satisfaction of scoring one quick point over the suave Mariano.

"Yours was a ginger beer, I think, sir?"

The waiter glanced inquiringly at Mariano, who nodded and confirmed: "Stone ginger beer." He intercepted Temple's quick glance of surprise. "A drink is perhaps like a prophet. It seldom has honour in its own country. If my business in England fails I shall make a fortune importing stone ginger beer into Spain."

Temple laughed and repeated his own order to the waiter. Mariano was emboldened to return to the delicate topic.

"It is not untrue what the papers have been saying – that you have already been approached by Sir Graham Forbes about the Tyler mystery?"

"There is some truth in it," Temple admitted. He felt sure that Mariano had something on his mind, something which he was diffident about mentioning. There would be no advantage in high-hatting him, as he was sure Vosper had done.

"She was one of my favourite girls, Betty Tyler. A really good kid." The Spanish accent and idiom tended to wear off as the interview warmed up. Mariano had an almost perfect command of English, but he found it helped him professionally to preserve the foreign flavour of his conversation. "As a matter of fact I was a little worried about her even before she asked to be transferred to Oxford."

"Oh? Why was that?"

Mariano switched on his professional smile; he rose a few inches from his chair and bowed to a lady who was passing behind Temple's back. He saw her mirrored on the wall above the Spaniard's head – a tall slim girl whose photograph was a regular feature of the society magazines.

"About three months ago," Mariano went on, switching his attention back to Temple. "She asked me for several days off. She told me she was going to a house party at Seldon Chase – you know, of course, that Westeral is the son of Lord Seldon. Naturally I consented. It does not do my business any harm if my employees are friendly with the aristocracy, but I was just a little disappointed when I found that Betty had been telling me a story. It was quite by chance that I was called to Paris myself on business."

Mariano smiled confidingly at Temple. "You understand that my business does not always take place in offices and shops. On Sunday afternoon I attended the race meeting at Auteuil – you know, a very fashionable crowd goes to watch the Grand Prix du Printemps. I saw Betty Tyler standing close to the entrance of the Private Enclosure. She hadn't seen me so I just went past and didn't say anything to her about it. But it was a disappointment when one trusts someone—"

"There may have been a perfectly simple explanation," Temple suggested. "Perhaps her plans were changed and she went to Paris with Westeral."

Mariano shook his head sadly.

"When I asked her about her holiday Betty spoke about the house party and tried to make me believe she had been there." Mariano shrugged and sipped at his stone ginger beer. "Perhaps I was mistaken. Perhaps I didn't see Betty Tyler in Paris."

"This girl you saw. Was she alone?"

"She was alone, yes. But she was looking about her as if she expected to be joined by someone. She was not the kind of girl who would feel comfortable to be alone at a race meeting in Paris."

In spite of what he had said, Temple thought to himself, Mariano was convinced that the girl he had seen was indeed Betty Tyler.

"Did you mention any of this to the police when they questioned you?"

Mariano met Temple's eyes blandly. There was a twinkle in his own.

"No. I did not."

"Had you any reason for withholding the information?"

"None whatever," Mariano answered smoothly. "It was just that they did not ask me that particular question."

Soon afterwards Temple pleaded the excuse of his fictitious dinner engagement. Mariano rose too and accompanied him up to the street. Before they parted he promised to let Temple know if he learnt anything that seemed to have a bearing on the case. In spite of the latter's mild protestations he had assumed that Paul Temple was now fully involved in the Tyler mystery.

"Well," Steve called out as soon as she heard Temple come in. "What did you think of him?"

She was in her bedroom, dressing for dinner after a hot bath. Temple changed his outdoor shoes for a pair of slippers and went to sit on the bed and talk to her while she completed her toilet.

"He was quite different from what I'd been expecting from your description. Actually I rather liked him. We got on quite well together. He tried to retain my services at any fee I liked to mention."

"Darling, you should have accepted."

"He's rather difficult to make out. He's a rogue in many ways, of course, but I somehow can't see him mixed up in anything really shady."

"Of course not. Otherwise why should he have asked you to investigate the case? Personally I think he's absolutely sweet. I'm glad you two got along quite well together. Did he tell you anything sensational?"

"Not exactly sensational. But he did produce a rather odd story about Betty Tyler."

Temple repeated the account Mariano had given him of his encounter with Betty in Paris.

"I wonder why she should lie about a thing like that," Steve said thoughtfully. "We've heard about gentlemen slipping secretly over to Paris, haven't we? It's rather rare for girls. Do you suppose that's when she collected the scarf she was strangled with? Oh, Paul! Perhaps the person she was waiting for was Jane Dallas. Remember she had a similar scarf."

"That's an interesting possibility. We might check up with Vosper on that – did Jane Dallas have a passport and does it record a trip to France about three months ago? Always assuming that your friend Mariano was not leading me up the garden path."

"If he leads anyone up the garden path, darling, it won't be you, I can assure you." Steve stood up and presented her back. "Now you can do my buttons, please."

The proofs of Temple's new book had just come from the publishers and he brought them into the drawing room after dinner and settled down with them in his own chair. He hoped he was going to be able to devote three uninterrupted hours to correcting them. It was with considerable impatience that he heard Charlie go to answer a ring at the front door and then come and knock at the drawing room door.

"There's a gentleman here would like to see Mr. Temple."

Steve said: "Who is it, Charlie?"

"Mr. Brooks."

"Brooks. The same gentleman was here the other day?"

"No. This is another one."

Steve raised her eyebrows inquiringly at her frowning husband. He put his work down and sighed.

"Oh, I suppose so."

"Ask him to come in, Charlie."

Temple contrived to have a civilised expression on his face when the visitor was shown in and Steve was as usual the charming, unruffled hostess. The new Brooks marched straight into the depths of the room, radiating goodwill and boyish enthusiasm. By contrast to his willowy namesake he was an open air, mackintoshy kind of man with a lean jaw and wavy fair hair.

"Forgive me bursting in on you like this. You don't know me from Adam, of course. My name's Brooks – Garry Brooks."

"Ah, yes," Temple said. "The man at the British Embassy in Paris."

"That's it. I flew over today to see poor old Stephen. They whistled him off at a moment's notice the other day—"

"Yes, we only heard about that this morning," Steve said. "I hope it's nothing very serious."

"Luckily they got it in time." Garry Brooks' eyes were working overtime, taking in every detail of the Temple's drawing room. "I'm afraid Stephen rather imposed on your kindness. He told me that you had kindly consented to act as couriers and bring a little parcel out to me."

"Yes, your cigars. It's a good thing you thought of

calling on us. It turns out that we're not going to Paris after all. If you hang on a second I'll get the parcel for you."

Temple left the room and while they were waiting Steve tried to make her visitor feel at ease. He was surprisingly jumpy for a diplomat. She thought that perhaps he was allergic to women for he was obviously relieved when Temple reappeared carrying the still loosely wrapped parcel.

"There you are. You'll find the seal is broken and one cigar is missing, but that's not because I've been raiding your property. It was a device of your brother's for thwarting the French customs and excise."

Garry laughed as he took the parcel. "I know about that. Stephen absolutely revels in that sort of thing."

"What hospital is he in?" Temple asked, initiating the sort of polite conversation that is aimed at making guests feel they may stay a little longer.

"Oh, the West Middlesex actually. Just an appendix, you know. Doesn't sound much now it's over, but the doctor told me that if they'd been an hour later, the thing would have burst."

"How awful!" Steve exclaimed. "Do give him our very best wishes, won't you?"

"I will indeed."

"How long are you staying over here?" Temple asked.

"Just a couple of days, I expect. The Embassy are rather

tight on leave, I'm afraid. Still, now that one can fly so cheaply it's easier to nip over for these short visits."

"I'm afraid I'm rather conservative in that respect. I usually go by the night ferry. How long did your journey take, as a matter of interest?"

"Well." Garry Brooks pursed his lips and thought for a moment. "I left the Gare des Invalides this morning soon after ten and was at the hospital by two o'clock. That's four hours from door to door."

"As little as that," Temple murmured.

Garry Brooks glanced at his watch and buttoned his jacket.

"Well, I really must be getting along. So sorry to have barged in on you like this."

"Not at all," Steve assured him. "We were wondering what to do about the box of cigars."

Standing in front of the fireplace with her hands behind her back, Steve heard her husband conveying Garry Brooks out to the front door. An instant after it was closed, she was astonished to see him re-enter the room like a terrier on the scent. He made straight for the rack where the volumes of the London Telephone Directory were stored, picked out the last one and began feverishly to turn the pages.

"Paul, what on earth—?"

"Shh."

Temple was already dialling a number, holding his index finger on the open directory.

"Hello. Is that the West Middlesex Hospital? Is Dr. O'Day there by any chance? . . . He is? . . . Good. Would you ask him if he'd speak to Mr. Temple. It's rather urgent . . . Thank you."

Temple drummed with his fingers on the telephone table while he waited, and bent on Steve such a fierce and concentrated stare that she did not dare to breathe another word.

"O'Day? Temple here. I wonder if you'd do me a favour. I'd like to verify whether you've a patient in the West Middlesex called Brooks. . . . Yes. Stephen Brooks . . . I'll hold on."

There followed another four minutes of table drumming. Steve sat down.

"Yes, still here . . . There isn't? . . . No, that's all I wanted to know. Thank you very much. How are Mary and the boys? . . . Oh, splendid. Steve? She's in fine fettle. . . . Yes, we must some time. Goodbye."

Temple replaced the receiver and stood up. For the first time since the Tyler mystery had blown up he was wearing what she thought of as his bloodhound expression.

"Paul, what *is* all this about?"

"I haven't the vaguest idea, Steve, but someone is trying to take the mickey out of you and me. If that young man is employed at the British Embassy in Paris he gets a good deal more leave than he makes out. He was at Sonning the day we were."

"At Sonning! I don't remember seeing him."

"He took good care you shouldn't. I spotted him from the telephone booth just as you were coming back from powdering your nose. He did a fine imitation of Lot's wife when he saw you – then turned tail and legged it out of the place fast. He was very surprised indeed to see you. I'd give a lot to know what he looks like in a cap and goggles."

"You think he was the driver of the Triumph?"

"Can you think of any other reason why he should have been so startled to see us at 'The Dutch Treat'? He was probably confident that we were at that moment being scraped off the radiator of that brick lorry."

Steve shivered.

"You don't have to be so crude, Paul. Actually I can think of other reasons for him being surprised to see me at 'The Dutch Treat'."

"That's really beside the point. The fact remains that he was lying. He no more flew from Paris this morning than I did."

"But why did he lie? And what was the object of coming here to tell us all that rigmarole about brother Stephen?"

"Obviously because he wanted the cigars."

"And you gave them to him?"

Temple shook his head. Without answering he went through to his study. When he came back he had a box of cigars in his hand.

"These are the cigars Stephen Brooks gave me. I handed friend Garry a box of my own cigars minus one which I smoked last night after Vosper left."

CHAPTER FIVE

"Don't you see what this means, Steve? It's a link between the Tyler case and Stephen Brooks. Now I wonder what it is about these cigars that interests brother Garry. Let's have that standard lamp over by the table here."

Steve brought the lamp across until it was shining down directly onto the coffee table. Temple cleared everything else off the table, planted the cigar box in the middle and sat down in front of it. He opened it carefully, lifted the cigars out and placed them in a neat row on the shiny mahogany. Then he subjected the empty box to an exhaustive scrutiny, holding it up to the light so that he could see through the leaves of paper which folded over the cigars.

"Steve, would you take this box out to Charlie? Tell him to put a kettle on and steam the paper away from the wood. He'll know what to do. I want the paper intact. There may be something on the other side."

While she was gone, Temple began to examine the cigars, sniffing them and weighing them on the palm of his hand. All twenty-four of them were genuine Havanas. He began to take the bands off, peering to see if anything was written microscopically on the inside. The band of the tenth cigar refused to slip off. He took a razor blade knife from his waistcoat pocket and carefully slit the band. It still refused to budge. He began to lever it gently away from the cigar but as it came it dragged the outer surface of the tobacco with it. A band of adhesive material had been fixed round the cigar and the proper band replaced on top of it. Confident now of what he was doing, Temple ripped the band away. The cigar still hung precariously together, but a small pull severed the two ends.

In the centre a neat cylinder had been hollowed out. Temple drew from it a small curled-up square of dark shiny material. He put it carefully on the table and went to the door of Charlie's kitchen. Clouds of steam were already pouring from the electric kettle and his and Steve's heads were bent over the box.

"It's all right, Charlie. You needn't bother. If anyone calls I'm not at home."

Steve came running back to the drawing room after him.

"Have you found something, Paul?"

Temple nodded.

"You know that pocket viewer I use to look at colour photos. It was on my desk this morning. Where did you put it?"

"It's in one of the drawers. Shall I get it?"

Steve was already on her way to the study. It did not take her thirty seconds to find the viewer and bring it back.

"What is it, Paul? A piece of film?"

"Yes." Temple nodded towards the bisected cigar. "It was concealed in the centre of that cigar. Not a bad hiding place."

Steve picked up the cigar and examined it, while Temple slid the piece of 35 millimetre film into the viewer and switched on the light which illuminated it from underneath. He crouched down and stared at the film through the swivelled magnifying glass. Steve sat beside him, longing to be given a turn.

"What's it of, Paul?"

"Wait a sec."

Temple stared into the magnifier for a minute. Then he said: "By Timothy! What do you think of that, Steve?"

Steve took the viewer with alacrity.

"It looks like a section of map."

"That's what it is. What else do you see?"

"Ty Hir," Steve read out slowly. "Hut circles. Park Manor. What on earth language is that?"

"Bottom right hand corner," Temple prompted. "You see the village marked Davidstown? Just a little to the right there's a group of buildings."

"Crows Farm?"

"That's it. Just underneath there's a series of initials and figures. Haven't they been written on in ink?"

Following his directions, Steve was able to pick out the faint markings on the map. Someone had very neatly inked in: H.S. 2345—9/5.

"Yes. It's been written with a mapping pen, I should think. Does it make any sense to you?"

Reluctantly Steve surrendered the viewer to Temple, who peered through it again.

"Not at the moment, it doesn't. But there's one rather odd coincidence. The letters H.S. Can you think of anyone we know who has those initials?"

"Harry Shelford!" Steve breathed. "There can't be any possible connection."

"I don't see how there can be," Temple agreed. "The Brooks brothers are obviously involved in some extremely clandestine activity and thought it would be an amusing idea to use me as an unwitting courier."

"Davidstown. I wonder what part of the world that's in."

"Wales. Where else would you find the name Llanychlwydor? The Prescelly Hills must be just off this section of map. I can see the word Prescelly—"

"Never heard of them," Steve confessed without compunction.

"Well, you should have. That's where the stones for Stonehenge were brought from."

"A bit before my time."

Temple ignored the remark. He was again engrossed in the brightly illuminated section of map.

"I'm certain this is a photograph of the one-inch Ordnance Survey. I know we haven't any of the Welsh sheets but we have a full set of the quarter-inch. It might be on that."

A few minutes later Temple stabbed his finger on a point near the Pembrokeshire coast, a little to the east of Fishguard. "There it is! Now all we have to do is find the appropriate sheet of the one-inch survey."

Steve was staring at him with puckered brows.

"You really think there may be a connection, then?"

"To quote a remark of Sir Graham's: 'It's a line of investigation we can't afford to ignore'."

"You're going to tell him about this?"

Temple stood up and, began to walk slowly up and down the room.

"I don't think so. This may be a complete red herring and the police have enough on their hands as it is. But someone has an interest in Crows Farm – someone whose activities are so secret that he falls back on the sort of device spies used in wartime for transmitting messages."

"Those figures might be a code."

"Probably are – though nine stroke five is a common way of writing a date."

"The ninth of the fifth," Steve confirmed. "That's three days from now."

"And 2345 could possibly be a map reference. This probably indicates a meeting place."

"The only thing is – the west coast of Wales is a rather out-of-the-way place to meet anyone."

"That could have its advantages. Besides, Fishguard is only five hours from London by train—"

"Paul! I've got it!" Steve had jumped up in her excitement. "You know the way they use the twenty-four hour clock in railway time tables. 2345 could indicate a time of day."

"Eleven forty five p.m." Temple regarded his wife appreciatively. "Of course. Why didn't we think of it before? A quarter of an hour before midnight on the 9th May. If there is any connection between this and the Tyler mystery—"

Temple broke off, moved to the bookshelf and took out the A.A. manual.

"Davidstown. Davidstown. Here it is. 247 miles from London by road. That shouldn't take more than five hours in a decent car."

"Would you call the Frazer Nash a decent car?" Steve asked casually.

"Yes, I would."

"And you could tell me all about Stonehenge on the way."

"Yes," he agreed. "I could."

The following day was Sunday but nonetheless Sir Graham Forbes was at his desk in Scotland Yard. After drawing a blank at his house, Temple telephoned him there. He explained that he and Steve were leaving town for a few days to follow up a lead which they hoped might have some connection with the Tyler case. Sir Graham was curious but Temple told him they were only backing a hunch and might draw a complete blank.

"If Vosper is in, there are a couple of points I'd like to raise with him."

"He's gone down to Guildford. But I can pass on a message to him for you, Temple."

"Well – if you would—. First: would he check Jane Dallas' passport, if she has one, and find out whether she could have visited Paris about three months ago."

"Jane Dallas – Paris."

He could hear Sir Graham muttering the words as he wrote them down.

"Second: it might be interesting to check the movements of one Stephen Brooks, lately employed at the Anderson Gallery in Bond Street and of his brother Garry Brooks, whose address I don't know."

"I've got that," Sir Graham said a moment later. "Is there anywhere we can contact you while you're away?"

"I'll try and notify you of my address when we get there. I think we should be back on the tenth."

Temple wrote a brief note to Watson, his agent, telling him that he would be out of town for a few days and instructing him to stall on any offers that might come through. From a friend who was a great enthusiast on car rallies he managed to borrow the Ordnance Survey one-

inch sheet of North Pembrokeshire. What with one thing
and another, it was twelve o'clock before Charlie carried
the two suitcases down and stowed them in the boot of
the Frazer Nash.

"We'll leave you to hold the fort, Charlie," Temple said.
"Make sure you lock up well if you go out. I have a suspicion someone may try to burgle us in the not too distant
future. I'll try and let you know where we are in case there
are urgent messages."

Temple took the wheel himself for the first spell and
managed to get forty miles on the clock before lunch. They
stopped at a hotel a few miles outside Oxford, knowing that
the worst of the traffic was behind them. Steve took over
the driving for the first hour after lunch. She drove fast but
well and Temple abandoned himself to the kind of relaxation
which can only be experienced in a moving vehicle.

The spell of brilliant weather extended over the whole
of Britain. Even when they crossed the Welsh border and
approached the mountains the blue of the sky remained
unbroken. The Brecon Beacons wore a healthy haze which
was a good omen for the future. At Carmarthen they
forsook the A40 and Steve took the wheel again. Temple
refolded his Ordnance Survey map and prepared to direct
her along the minor roads which would bring them to the
village of Davidstown.

"We should be there by seven easily," he told her. "Drive
slowly. I want to get an idea of the country."

They were penetrating into a completely unspoiled agricultural district. The land was broken up into small fields by high, thick hedges or solidly constructed stone walls. Here and there chunky little farm houses, built of grey stone, seemed as much a part of the countryside as the trees and hills. People were not too blasé to come running out to stare at the car as it went rumbling gently past. They were happy, healthy and friendly – an eloquent testimony of how much England lost by the Industrial Revolution.

"Davidstown!" Steve shouted suddenly and there ahead of them was the first signpost pointing to their destination.

Before they reached it, the smooth rounded summits of the Prescelly Hills were rising on their left. The hills themselves seemed bare and windswept, but they were broken every now and then by the green tongue of a richly wooded valley, where trees flourished and an immense variety of wild flowers and life of every description teemed. Davidstown was a small township of perhaps a thousand-odd inhabitants. It was dominated by the ruins of a castle which had been one of the few Norman strongholds in the district. It possessed one inn, the "Crown and Anchor", which stood on the cross-roads at the centre of the town.

The landlord and his wife greeted the Temples with a welcome worthy of Pickwickian days. The room they were shown was dark, bare and as cold as a tomb, but spotlessly clean. A huge four poster bed loomed up in the darkness and the floor undulated to a deep ground-swell. The windows, starting at floor level, looked out on to a companionable piece of meadow where old car springs, discarded cart-wheels and broken bicycles lay rusting.

"This all right for you, Steve?"

Steve forced a courageous smile and gave the landlord and his wife the benefit of her charm.

"Yes. I think it's lovely. We might even stay here a day or two, Paul?"

"Just touring, are you?" the landlord inquired.

"Yes. I'm rather interested in Paleolithic remains. I believe this area is very rich in that sort of thing."

Steve shot her husband a look of surprise but preserved a straight face. The landlord's wife took her cue with enthusiasm.

"Yes, indeed, dear. We get a lot of archeologists coming down here. You know the stones they used building Stonehenge come from the Prescelly Hills."

"Indeed?" Temple answered with immense interest, while Steve covered her mouth with her hand and turned away.

The bar parlour of the "Crown and Anchor" was the focal point of Davidstown, but the dining room was as bleak as a base camp on the lower slopes of Everest. Steve and Temple sat enshrouded in a fragile silence while a still, small waiter, moving with intense care, brought them lukewarm soup, chops and apple tart.

They went to bed desperately early that night. There was nothing else to do. The last remark Steve made before she went to sleep was: "Someone's put a cold hot water bottle in my half of the bed."

"That's not a hot water bottle," Temple growled. "That's my foot."

At half-past six when the sun shining through the window woke them, they were surfeited with sleep. They had committed themselves to breakfast at eight-thirty, so Temple readily agreed to Steve's suggestion that they should go for a walk while the air was still fresh and crisp. Someone in the hotel was already astir. They could hear the soft thud of mats being beaten out against a wall at the back and the door was open. A lane leading uphill from the main street promised to take them quickly away from the houses.

Ten minutes later, they were looking down on the roofs of Davidstown from a height of a hundred feet or so. Steve stopped to gaze in rapture at the new-born lambs skipping about in the walled fields. The farm folk were already up and about. A tractor was moving slowly up the hill towards them, the glittering blades of a plough attached to its rear. The driver stopped just beside them and dismounted to open the gate into his field. As soon as Temple saw where he wanted to go he went quickly and opened the gate for him. The driver combined a nod of thanks with a touch of the forefinger to his cap. He turned in through the gate, stopped the tractor, cut his engine off and stepped down.

"That was very kind of you now, sir." He had the whole day ahead of him and was ready to spend ten minutes of it in talk. He was past forty but still fit and wiry. His face was burnt brick red by the weather and his eyes were as keen as a sailor's.

"Just on holiday, you are?"

They swung off into the usual patter. Temple brought the conversation round to archeological remains.

"I heard there were some very interesting cromlechs at Crows Farm. Do you know it at all?"

"Cromlechs at Crows Farm? No. I don't think you'll find anything much there." He spoke slowly with that pure enunciation of vowel sounds which makes English such a harmonious language on the tongues of the Welsh. "But if you want to go there it's not such a long walk. Five or six miles, perhaps. Look now, you can see it from here."

He took Temple's elbow, turned him towards the west and pointed out a group of buildings on the flank of a hill. They stood just about the spot where the fields ended and the upland moor began.

"Can you get up there by car?"

"Well, I don't know that the road is very good, dear. The place is empty now. It has been ever since the war. The Army requisitioned it for storing ammunition and one night there was a fire and most of the buildings were destroyed, you see."

"Mostly sheep farming round here, isn't it?"

"Sheep farming mostly, yes. But Mr. Tomlinson, he has a dairy herd. Supplies most of the milk for round here."

"It's a lovely bit of country," Steve interposed with genuine enthusiasm. The farmer turned to her with courtly politeness.

"Yes, ma'am. It is. And for educated people such as yourselves, it's very interesting. You've heard of Stonehenge, no doubt. . . ."

As they walked back to the hotel for breakfast, Steve said: "If anyone else tries to tell me about Stonehenge, I shall scream."

Monday breakfast was a more hearty meal than Sunday supper at the "Crown and Anchor". Steve and Temple felt greatly fortified as they drove out along the road that led to Crows Farm. They stopped about a mile from the farm itself and left the car in a small disused quarry where it was unlikely to attract attention. The track leading up to the farm was in good condition. It had been resurfaced when the Army took the place over and had not been much used by vehicles since. A faded, neglected notice a hundred yards from the buildings gave its aimless warnings:

"High Explosives. Danger. Keep out."

The buildings themselves were as the farmer had told them, shattered and derelict. They approached them with that curious hushed feeling which is induced by abandoned human dwellings. For how many people did memories of infancy evoke these trees and walls, the shapes of these hills? Beyond one shattered wall could be seen the fireplace of the main living room. It was open to the sky and wind, but on thousands of evenings it had been the focus of a hard working family after a day's labour in the fields.

"My guess is that this place was uninhabited even before the Army took over," Temple said. "It's the same all over these hills. The line of cultivation is gradually moving down as the people desert the country for the town."

They toured the outhouses, which were in better condition than the farmhouse itself. It seemed that they had been kept in use by an absentee farmer after the house had fallen into disrepair. In one outhouse they found a rusty child's pram, a wooden horse and broken scythe. In the yard lay a soldier's tin helmet with a jagged gash across the crown. A fire bucket which had once been painted red hung on a post near a rectangular patch of concrete. Small flies buzzed noisily about their business in the warm sun.

Steve shivered.

"I don't like this place, Paul. There's something spooky about it." Temple took her to a stone wall and pointed into a broad flat meadow where a healthy herd of rust coloured dairy cattle were cropping the grass.

"Nothing spooky about that. There must be some other way up from Tomlinson's place."

"How do you know that?"

"You can usually tell where cattle have passed, my dear Steve. The lane we came up was unsullied."

Temple shaded his eyes and stared back at the group of buildings.

"Whatever this place was used for in the past, it's a perfect secret meeting place now. I think we're on the track of something, Steve, and we ought to have some clue to it by midnight tonight. Let's see if we can find a place from which we can watch proceedings in reasonable comfort."

They began to walk up the hill at the back of the house and were soon on the edge of the moor which sloped away over the Prescelly Hills beyond. Here the closely cropped fields gave place to heather and low gorse. Whoever had farmed the land in days gone by had built a number of small, square stone pens along the wall here to shelter his sheep from the wind. They had tumbled down since those days and grass had grown over them. But they formed comfortable little hollows lined with springy turf.

"What a perfect place for a picnic!" Steve exclaimed.

"And a perfect place for watching the farm. No skyline behind us and plenty of jagged gaps in the wall. This is where we shall come tonight."

On the drive back into Davidstown, Steve pointed out to Temple something they had missed on the way out; the white painted gates of a prosperous farm bearing the name Brynfynnon in neat letters. Temple drove slowly past and they caught a quick glimpse of a very fine house overlooking an extensive stretch of park land. Tomlinson apparently bred horses as well as dairy cattle. Three very fine thoroughbreds were being exercised by their stable lads on the soft, rolling turf.

"Tomlinson seems to be making his dairy farm pay," Temple commented.

They had both worked up a useful thirst during the walk up the hill to Crows Farm. Several cars were parked in the space opposite the hotel and the sounds emerging from the bar were companionable. It was clear that the Saloon Bar of the "Crown and Anchor" was a focal point in Davidstown life.

"What about a drink before lunch?" Temple suggested and Steve nodded readily.

"I'd love one."

The landlord himself was behind the bar. As usual when strangers enter a country pub a brief hush fell on the conversation. All the occupants of the bar were men and they were standing at the counter in a compact group. To judge by their leather leggings, knobbly sticks and battered hats they were mostly farmers. Steve immediately realised that she was going to be the only woman amongst a dozen men, but the landlord greeted them cheerfully and suggested they might sit at a secluded little alcove near the window.

"And what can I give you to drink?"

"Two glasses of your best bitter, please."

The landlord glanced at Steve in surprise, but she smiled at him reassuringly and he went off to pull on his levers. The men at the bar had struck up their conversation again, but their eyes constantly swung with interest towards Steve. Temple thought that the tall man who formed the centre of the group seemed to be a cut above the rest. They did not treat him precisely as a squire, but they showed him a good deal of deference and made a point of listening whenever he had something to say. It came as no surprise when he heard one of them address him as Mr. Tomlinson. Over the edge of his glass of beer he studied the owner of Brynfynnon and Crows Farm with interest. In contrast to the lean, hawk-faced men who were with him he was a big, jovial fellow with a tendency to spread around the midriff.

His voice was educated and quietly pitched, but strong enough to carry through a conversation.

Suddenly Temple found himself looking straight into the other man's eyes. He immediately excused himself and came over to their table.

"I'm Ronald Tomlinson. I hear you've been making enquiries about Crows Farm. Can I help you at all? I own the place."

Temple got to his feet and introduced himself and Steve. Tomlinson shook hands warmly with the bluff friendliness of the countryman.

Temple said: "We've been rather bitten with this Ancient Britain stuff on television, my wife and I. Someone told us that there were very interesting hut circles and cromlechs in this district and I thought I remembered them mentioning Crows Farm."

It was a thin excuse, Temple realised, but Tomlinson appeared to take it seriously.

"If there's anything of that sort up there it's news to me," he laughed. "Still you're welcome to come up and have a look some time. I'd be glad to show you round. How long do you propose staying here?"

"Three or four days, I expect. It rather depends."

"Well, look here, you must come along to my place for a drink, some time. I'm at Brynfynnon Farm. Anyone will tell you where it is."

"That's very kind of you. Will you join us for a drink now?"

"I won't, thank you. But please sit down."

Temple accepted his invitation. Though he had refused the offer of a drink, Tomlinson was reluctant to leave them. He remained, leaning one hand on the table, keeping his hearty smile going.

"My daughter's a great fan of yours. She must have read all your books, I should think. She'd be more than pleased if you'd come out and autograph one or two. Just drop in before lunch or dinner, any day. We keep open house at Brynfynnon."

"That's most kind of you," Steve said and Temple murmured: "We'll try to do that."

Almost as soon as he had left them Tomlinson took his departure, lifting a hand to them as he opened the street door.

"News travels fast around here," Steve observed softly. "Rather an unusual man to find in these parts."

"Yes. I wonder why he was so much on edge."

"Was he?"

"Didn't you notice the way he kept stroking the back of his neck? It's nearly always a sign of nerves. He seems friendly enough, but I wouldn't like to make an enemy of him – he's pretty ruthless at the core, I should think."

"He thinks he's rather good-looking," Steve remarked. "But he hasn't half the distinction of the nice farmer we talked to this morning. What about lunch? I'm famished."

The morning sun had been stronger than Steve realised. After lunch she complained of a slight headache. Temple suggested that she should lie down for an hour or two.

"It won't do any harm to store up a few hours' credit sleep. You'll need it for our midnight vigil."

"What are you going to do?"

"I shall drive into Cardigan. I wasn't able to cash a cheque before we left and I want to make some arrangements about money."

*

Steve's headache was better by the evening, but Temple's trip to Cardigan had afflicted him with a terrible thirst. He consulted his watch every five minutes and the moment opening time came he had Steve down in the bar.

"This is very unlike you, Paul," she observed when he had ordered the third round of drinks. "You used to say that a pint of beer was all you could stomach at a time. Why do we have to keep sitting on this hard bench? My—"

"Sh," Temple cautioned her as the landlord approached with the tray. "Can't a man have a thirst without his wife nagging him?"

It was twenty to seven when there was a slight commotion behind the bar. The landlady had come in and was talking urgently to her husband. After listening to her for a moment he called across the parlour.

"Mr. Temple, it's telegrams on the line for you. I told them you were here but they wouldn't wait to give you the message personally. My daughter's taking it down now."

"I'll come," Temple said and with a muttered apology to Steve crossed the room.

Before he could reach the door the daughter of the house appeared behind her mother.

"I'm afraid this isn't very good news for you, Mr. Temple."

A complete silence fell over the bar. Every customer's eyes were on Temple as he took the sheet of paper. He read it through twice without any change of expression. Then he carried it over to Steve and put it in front of her.

"Paul! How awful! The diamond ear-rings you gave me for my birthday."

"Take it easy, darling. We are insured."

"I wonder what else they've taken. All my jewellery was in that drawer."

"There's only one thing for it. We shall have to get back to town right away."

Temple returned to the bar counter.

"I'm afraid we're going to have to leave you at rather short notice. Our home in London was burgled today."

The landlord and his lady nodded. They had already received a whispered précis of the news from their daughter.

"Is it necessary for you to go back tonight itself? Driving in the dark will not be very agreeable."

"There's nothing else for it. Only we can tell what has been taken. I need hardly say I'm very sorry we've had to cut our holiday short. If you'll prepare my bill I'd like to settle it in a few minutes. Of course I'll pay for tonight's lodging."

"Indeed you will not," the landlady put in. "We are not people to profit from the misfortunes of others."

"Well, if you put it like that— Come on, Steve. You and I have got to get packed in record time."

Accompanied by the murmured sympathies of the customers in the "Crown and Anchor", Steve and Temple left their unfinished drinks and climbed the narrow staircase to their bedroom.

In less than half an hour their hastily packed bags were carried down to the cobbled yard and stowed in the car. Temple fancied he saw a tear of sympathy in the eye of their landlady as she waved them goodbye. He began to feel a downright cad.

"If only they'd taken anything else but my ear-rings," Steve said sadly as they accelerated out of Davidstown. "You said to Charlie that you thought we might be burgled. How did you know? Where you expecting someone to try and take Stephen Brooks' box of cigars?"

"Relax, Steve. That telegram was a phoney. I telephoned Charlie this afternoon and told him to send it. I wanted to get us out of Davidstown so that Tomlinson and everyone else would think we'd returned to town."

Steve was silent for a full minute.

"That was a rotten trick," she said at last. "You needn't have brought my diamond ear-rings into it."

"That bit was Charlie's idea, but I must say I think it was a good one. You could never have acted the part so well."

"Wait till I see Master Charlie," Steve murmured between her teeth.

"You've one consolation. I've found us a very comfortable pub to stay in in Cardigan. If we have to hang around for a day we may as well do it in comfort. And I made a special point of asking for a warm hot water bottle for your feet."

CHAPTER SIX

Temple had nothing else to occupy his mind all next day and his thoughts worked their way again and again over the Tyler mystery. He was chafing at the delay, wondering whether important developments were taking place up in London while he and Steve were down in Wales on what might turn out to be a wild goose chase. For if the piece of film had never reached its destination would the appointment be kept? And if it was known that Temple had switched the boxes of cigars the whole plan might have been changed.

It was hard to believe with confidence that the derelict buildings up on the Prescelly Hills would provide any key to the murder of Betty Tyler and Jane Dallas. Temple reassured himself by thinking that in this unusual case events and people which appeared to have no possible connection with each other were linked by some invisible thread. Stephen Brooks, for instance, and the incident of the cigars. His behaviour had admittedly been unconventional but had it not been for one chance Temple would have forgotten him as soon as the cigars were off his hands. Why had Stephen Brooks faked a sudden operation and illness? Was it because he wanted to disappear for a few days or – and here Temple stopped in his pacing – was he already dead?

Then there was Mariano. He had wanted to engage Temple, he said, to create a certain impression in the minds of the public. He might equally well have intended to create that impression in other minds as well – Vosper's or Sir Graham Forbes' or even Temple's own. None the less Temple felt about Mariano rather as he did about Harry Shelford. He was a bit of a rogue but not the kind who gets mixed up in murder.

"'But soft you now'," Temple said to himself and looked towards Steve, sitting on the edge of the bed, filing her nails. She laughed, stood up and came towards him.

"Darling, what it is? Why the fierce expression?"

He put a hand behind her head and caressed the nape of her neck.

"I was just thinking that it is dangerous to say that anyone is incapable of murder."

"Who were you thinking of?"

"Myself."

"You?"

Steve searched the depths of Temple's eyes.

"Yes. When we so nearly had that crash on the Bath Road I had a momentary vision of your head being crushed against the dashboard."

"Darling," Steve whispered. "You're trembling."

"I'm afraid it makes me rather angry. I think that if I

ever found out who the driver of that Triumph was I'd be capable of killing him."

They were both relieved when the waiting was over and it was time to start for Crows Farm. Steve had been put in charge of the catering and had asked for some sandwiches and coffee which she packed into a cheap knapsack. There was also room in it for Temple's torch, night glasses and a small ground sheet from the car. The hotel manager, believing them to be a honeymoon couple with still romantic ideas, swallowed the story that they were going to watch the sunset from a hill in Snowdonia and agreed to lend them a key to the door.

The sun was due to set at 9.32. They agreed that it would be best to get up to Crows Farm in the gloaming.

As they walked up the hill by the same track as the previous day the sun touched the horizon. They stopped to rest and watch it sink out of sight. A thick veil of lead coloured mist, melting gradually through pink to the pale blue of the high sky, hung over the west. Behind it the sun was a dull, pulsating ball of fire. Seeming to move in jerks it vanished section by section, the last segment of the elipse lingering for just a second extra.

It was the moment which the dwellers in town miss – that indescribably eerie transition from day to night. All time seemed to be present now. Looking back towards the Prescelly Hills Temple knew why the men of the Iron Age had timed their religious ceremonies by the rising and setting of the sun. In the fields the lambs suddenly panicked and began bleating for their mothers. Innumerable small animals, knowing that the hawks had gone to rest, crept from their holes.

As they moved on Steve put her arm in Temple's. She had changed into operational dress; French-cut corduroy slacks, fur-lined boots and a thick woolly pullover with a hood that pulled up over her head. The first star was already out when they arranged their things in the hideout, as they called it.

"Those friendly cows have been taken away," Steve said, standing up on tip-toe to see into the meadow. "It all seems rather bleak and deserted without them."

"They're in one of the fields near Brynfynnon." Temple was standing up, inspecting the countryside through his glasses. "That may be so as to have them handy for milking in the morning. On the other hand—"

"What?"

"Nothing. Shall we eat while there's still some daylight?"

"Yes, let's."

Steve squatted on the soft grass and began laying out sandwiches and a half bottle of red wine which she had brought as a surprise.

"I thought it would help to keep us warm, and we can hold the coffee in reserve till later."

It was dark when they finished eating and there was

still an hour to wait. A three-quarter moon was already well up in the sky and as their eyes grew accustomed to the darkness they were able to see the grey humps of the now silent sheep, lying about the lower fields. The farm buildings themselves cast jet shadows and their outlines were more sinister than ever.

"If nothing happens I shall feel rather responsible," Steve said an hour later. She had fallen naturally into a whisper. "It's just on eleven forty-five."

In the trees below an owl hooted. The air was so still that they could hear the engine of a car moving along the main road in the valley, and occasionally glimpse the white sheet of light thrown by its headlights. It slowed and the beams of light swung in a huge arc across the sky. Almost at once they were extinguished.

"I think it's coming up here," Temple said and groped for his night glasses.

The sound of the car changing gear for the steep climb to the farm was quite distinct. Very soon they saw its twin sidelights between the high banks of the track they had come up. The driver was using moonlight to see his way. Clearly he did not wish to attract more attention to himself than necessary, though it was unlikely that the sleeping farms and hamlets were watching the Prescelly Hills at this hour of the night.

"We were right," Steve whispered exultantly.

Temple had his glasses trained on the car as it stopped

close to the farm buildings. The engine died and both front doors opened. From the driver's side emerged Tomlinson, rather more respectably dressed than when he had been in the "Crown and Anchor". From the other side stepped more carefully a man whom Temple had not seen before. His face was turned for a moment towards the two watchers as he spoke to Tomlinson across the bonnet of the car. He was a good-looking man aged about thirty-six or -seven and somehow gave the impression of having recently come from the West End of London. His hair was glossy and carefully combed, his black moustache trimmed to a shape, his camel hair coat unbuttoned but held by a belt loosely knotted at the front.

Both men walked into the shadow of the buildings and disappeared.

"Who was it?" Steve whispered.

"Tomlinson and a man I've never seen before."

Half an hour went by and nothing happened. But for the car standing there, its chromium glistening in the white light, they would have believed that the pair had gone.

"What the devil are they up to?" Temple grunted. "It's getting on for half past."

"Perhaps they're just having a secret meeting."

"They needn't have come up to this forsaken spot just for a cosy chat. They must be waiting for someone else."

"I wish he'd hurry up then. My feet are frozen."

Temple endured it for another forty minutes. Then he stood up.

"I'm going down there to have a look around."

"Paul, wait. You don't know where they are. . . ."

But Temple had already gone. Within ten yards he was absorbed by the shadow of the stone wall. It was easy going as far as the buildings themselves. He was able to follow a line of shadow all the way. When the wall ended, though, he had to take a chance and cross a patch of grass full in the light of the moon.

He tried the farm house first, because that was where the pair had seemed to go. It was difficult to avoid tripping over fallen stones and every now and then he had to duck past a great gap where the wall had caved in. He listened for several minutes but could not detect even the sound of breathing.

He decided to try the outbuildings and searched the ground for a covered line of approach. It meant either crossing an open back yard or making a long detour by a hedge. He decided on the latter and was half way there when one foot sank into a soft morass. He withdrew it with a squelching noise. After that his left foot felt very much colder.

The outbuildings were built on three sides of a rectangle and a wall with a gated gap in the middle formed the fourth. He crouched in the shadow of this wall, wondering if he could chance going through the gate.

Just above his head, no more than a few feet away, it seemed, someone sighed noisily.

"If he doesn't come soon I'm going to give up. The message probably went astray. I think you were crazy to trust Brooks to handle a thing like that."

The voice was Tomlinson's, but he sounded a good deal less sure of himself now than in the bar of the "Crown and Anchor".

"He'll come all right. He knew it was arranged for some time tonight in any case. You just keep your shirt on. We've been through a lot for this. I'm not going to have everything spoiled simply because you've no patience."

The other man's tone was muffled by the wall. Temple guessed that he was sitting down somewhere on the other side. The smoke from Tomlinson's pipe was drifting over Temple's head. The farmer had only to glance down at the shadows below him to see the outline of a human form. Temple did his best to keep his head down and his hands out of sight, lest their whiteness should attract attention.

"It's no good trying to throw blame on me, Davis. I'm taking a risk by letting you use this place for the rendezvous; if anything goes wrong suspicion is going to fall on me. What was that chap Temple doing, nosing about down in Davidstown? That's what I want to know."

To Temple's relief Tomlinson took his hands off the wall and turned back to his companion.

"I wish you'd shut up, Tomlinson. I tell you he'll be here

and that should be good enough for you. Now for God's sake stop belly-aching."

The other man's voice was sharp but Tomlinson seemed to take the rebuke lying down. As Temple moved away he heard him mutter.

"I still think we should have arranged to meet at Mick's."

Then he froze as the two men came out through the gate. They walked within a few yards of him and went towards the farm house proper, still arguing away in low voices.

Temple worked his way back towards the hideout. He had learnt enough to justify waiting longer and one very interesting tit-bit besides. He thought he would prove Steve unjustified in her fears for his safety by coming up on her unawares. Keeping low he approached the hideout noiselessly, put his head over the top of the wall and looked inside.

The small space was empty. The ground sheet and remains of their supper were there, but no sign of Steve.

"Steve!"

He whispered her name, but there was no answer. Nor was there any sign of her nearby. Temple's annoyance turned to disquiet. He knew that she was quite capable of coming down to the buildings to see what he was up to. He glanced at his watch and saw that he had been away nearly an hour. As if to emphasize his aloneness a faint breeze came in from the sea, making a rushing noise through the gorse and heather.

"Steve!"

He risked calling her name a little louder, then, receiving no answer, decided to go back to the buildings and try and find her. In his haste he moved with less caution than before. Breaking clear of the protection of the wall which gave him his line of approach to the farm he almost betrayed himself to Davis and Tomlinson. They had left the farm and were moving towards the meadow where the dairy herd had been grazing. Davis was carrying a large torch in his hand.

When they had passed, Temple ransacked the outhouses and the farmhouse, repeatedly calling Steve's name in a soft voice. There was not a trace of her.

Thoroughly exasperated and alarmed he returned to the hideout. Steve was sitting on the ground sheet calmly sipping coffee with both hands wrapped round the mug.

"There you are. You've been a long time."

"Steve, where have you been? I've been searching everywhere for you."

"I didn't see why I should sit here freezing to death so I decided to do a little investigating on my own. Have some coffee. It's lovely and warm."

"I wish you wouldn't do these things to me. I suppose it's no use telling you that we're investigating a murder – m-u-r-d-e-r."

Steve handed him the cup of steaming coffee. The rebuke was running off her back like water off a duck's. She was pleased with herself.

"I think I'm rather good at stalking. Those men went within a few yards of me and never saw me."

"Where on earth were you?"

"Down by the meadow where those nice cows were. You know it's a funny thing but I'm sure there wasn't that big gap in the hedge between the two fields yesterday. Perhaps that's why they won't let the cows come up here any more. Did you find out anything?"

"Yes. They're definitely expecting someone else, though Tomlinson is getting very impatient. He made one rather significant remark: he said 'We should have met at Mick's'."

"Listen—" Steve put a hand out and touched his arm. "There's another car coming."

Temple put his head on one side. The sound of an engine pulsed through the silent night air.

"That's not a car. It's a plane. Look! Down in the meadow."

From the meadow below a pencil of light shone up into the darkness. The sound, growing rapidly in volume, was suddenly identifiable as coming from over the hill behind them.

"Give me the glasses, Steve, quick!"

The plane was distinct for a moment as it flew across the line of the moon. It was a small machine, similar to the type used in artillery reconnaissance. The pilot had spotted Davis' torch and was circling over the farm buildings.

"Paul, he's going to land."

"Yes. I was half expecting this. All those preparations seemed to indicate the landing of a plane. Let's try and get a little closer. We should be able to reach the edge of the meadow."

The pilot was anxious to make certain of his landing ground. He flew low over the area several times before turning away to the east to make his run in. Temple and Steve had time to reach the hedge surrounding the field before he glided in, bounced over the ground, passing through the newly made gap in the hedge, and came to rest a hundred yards away. While the engine still ticked over, the door of the cockpit opened and a man jumped down. He stood clear of the aircraft and waved to the pilot. The machine turned in a circle and stood, poised for a moment, aimed at the gap in the hedge. Its engine roared at full throttle, it raced forward and just after it had passed through the gap its wheels lifted off the ground.

It banked away towards the east, skimming the top of the hills. In a few seconds the noise of the engine was blanketed by the rising ground.

Temple had his glasses trained on the man who had alighted from the aircraft. Davis and Tomlinson were hurrying forward to meet him as he strolled towards them.

Steve whispered: "Paul, can you see who it is?"

"No. He's wearing a hat and his coat collar's turned up."

They saw the new arrival greet Davis and Tomlinson. He turned for a moment to look after the departing plane and the brilliant moonlight caught his face. Temple gave an exclamation of surprise and handed the glasses to Steve.

"By Timothy, we were right, Steve! It's our old friend Harry Shelford."

Steve and Temple reached London the following afternoon. They had moved out of Crows Farm as soon as possible after Davis, Tomlinson and Shelford had left in the former's car. Immediately on reaching the Cardigan Hotel, Temple had knocked up the porter and put through a trunk call to Sir Graham Forbes' private house, warning him that Harry Shelford was in Pembrokeshire. While he and Steve snatched a few hours' sleep, the police of five counties were alerted, but when Temple telephoned again in the morning it was to hear that they had drawn a complete blank. Davis and Shelford had vanished into thin air.

"I think you ought to get back as soon as you can," Sir Graham had said. "There have been one or two interesting developments while you've been away."

Charlie seemed unusually pleased to see the Temples back. They soon discovered the reason why.

"That telephone hasn't stopped ringing since lunch-time," he complained as he dumped their suitcases in the hall. "I haven't had a chance to sit down or anything."

"Any message from Sir Graham?"

"Yes. He phoned to say he'd call in about tea time. Inspector Vosper himself was round only about half an hour ago, wondering if you'd got back yet."

Charlie jerked his thumb at the pile of letters on the hall table. On top was the distinctive format of a cable envelope.

"You've seen that, of course."

Temple sliced the envelope open and grunted as he read the contents.

"Who's it from, Paul?"

"Pasterwake. He's changed his plans again. Apparently he expects to arrive in London within the next twenty-four hours and hopes to receive me at the Dorchester."

"Don't these film magnates ever make up their minds?"

Steve was inquisitively looking through the envelopes. "This one's a bill, I'll bet. You'd better take care of it."

Temple glanced at the two-penny stamp and opened the flap. It contained a statement from the Anderson Galleries, Old Bond Street, for the sum of forty guineas.

"Well," Temple commented. "Mr. Brooks' indisposition, whatever form it may take, has not affected the efficiency of the accounts department."

*

Sir Graham arrived on the stroke of four and within a few minutes had taken up his favourite position in front of the fireplace.

"Now then," he started, fixing Steve and her husband with an admonishing stare, "I expect a full testimony and account of this mysterious visit to Wales. What on earth started you off on that scent?"

He listened with concentration, completely oblivious of the cup of tea cooling on the mantelpiece behind his head, while Temple explained how the discovery of the film negative in Stephen Brooks' box of cigars had led them to Crows Farm.

"I didn't want to say anything about it in case we'd gone off on a fool's errand, Sir Graham. But the gamble paid off all right. Any sign of Shelford and Davis since I spoke to you this morning?"

"I'm afraid not. The police of the entire country are on the watch for them, but I'm afraid we've lost them. Master Tomlinson, of course, is innocently farming his acres as if nothing had happened. We've taken your advice and left him strictly alone."

He turned to take a sip from his teacup, found it was cold and put it down with a grimace. Steve moved swiftly and unobtrusively to pour him a fresh cup.

"What intrigues me," he went on, "is this Mick business. You've no idea what that means?"

Temple shook his head.

"I hoped it might ring a bell with you or Vosper—"

"Vosper knows about a hundred Micks who've been up to no good at one time or another and there are a few thousand more on the records at Central Office. Still it's a part of the puzzle which may fit in with something else later. Thank you, Steve." Forbes downed his tea with a perfunctory gulp and returned the cup to Steve.

"We're checking up on Tomlinson, of course, though personally I can't see a successful farmer as a potential accessory to murder. Still, in these days of enlightened crime you never can tell. It all seems a very long way from the murders of Tyler and Dallas."

"There's a connection somewhere, I'm sure," Temple said with conviction. "The fact that both girls worked for Mariano may not be the only significant link between them. There's some other underlying factor – something very much deeper than we thought at first."

"By the way, Vosper's man located Jane Dallas' passport. She has been to France but not in the last two years."

"That disposes of that," Temple remarked and though Sir Graham cocked an inquiring eyebrow at him he would say no more.

"No news of my friend Brooks?"

"No. I haven't had a report from Vosper on him yet. He's pretty pushed, you know."

"Paul," Steve said as soon as the door had closed on their visitor, "there was one very important point you didn't mention to Sir Graham – about Mariano seeing Betty Tyler in Paris when she was supposed to be at Seldon Chase."

"I know. I left that out on purpose. I thought I'd like to have a talk with the Honourable George about that weekend before Vosper takes the cream off the milk."

George Westeral was surprised but affable when Temple announced himself on the telephone next morning, and asked if there was any chance of their meeting for a talk.

"I'd like to very much," he said. "Unfortunately I have to go down to the country this morning. My father is a permanent invalid, you know, and he's having one of his bad spells."

"I'm sorry to hear that. You'll be at Seldon Chase, I suppose?"

"Yes, that's right."

"Well, look here. If I happen to be down in that part of the country would you mind if I dropped in to see you?"

"Well – er – not at all." Westeral was either too surprised or well bred to offer any objection. "We shall always be very glad to see you, but I warn you, it's rather bleak and stark."

"That's very kind of you. I hope we shall be able to meet soon."

Having achieved what he wanted, Temple said his goodbyes quickly and rang off. He picked the account from Anderson's Galleries off the side of his desk, took his cheque book from the drawer and phoned for a Radio Cab to take him to Bond Street.

Another picture, a system of polyhedra representing a complacent but repellent female form, occupied the place of honour in the window of Anderson's Galleries. On entering Temple was waylaid by a young and very earnest person who appeared to be just emerging from the art student stage. His regulation dark suit seemed to sit uneasily on him and Temple could imagine him rushing home when office hours were over to change into crushed corduroys, a brilliant check shirt and sandals. He stared at Temple with intensity, recollected the formula and said:

"Good morning, sir. Can I help you?"

"I rather wanted to see Mr. Brooks if he's in this morning."

"Well, actually, sir, Mr. Brooks is away just now. But if there's anything I can do for you – my name's Swinstead—"

"It was really a personal matter. You've no idea where Mr. Brooks is or when he'll be back?"

The young man shook his head.

"None at all, I'm afraid. The sooner the better, as far as I'm concerned. I was sent up here at short notice a few days ago. Bond Street's not my cup of tea at all. I'm usually at the Chelsea shop."

"Oh, you have several branches, have you?"

"Dear me, yes." Swinstead looked at Temple reprovingly. "We're very well known in a number of places."

"But this is the main gallery – the headquarters of the firm, I mean?"

"Gracious, no!" The young man suppressed a giggle. "Chelsea's the depot shop, as you might say. This is only a sort of façade – so to speak. This is where we reckon to sell off more conventional paintings to people who have more money than taste."

"I see," Temple said and decided that for the time being he would leave his account with Anderson's Galleries unpaid. "And you've no idea where I would find Mr. Brooks?"

"I don't think you'll find him at all. I heard some story about a mysterious illness – it wouldn't surprise me. Still, I can't talk, I hardly know the man."

Swinstead glanced guiltily at the silent pictures as if he were afraid they might repeat his veiled insinuations about Brooks, then flashed at Temple a conspiratorial smile.

"Have you met his brother at all?"

"Brother?" Swinstead repeated blankly, "I didn't know he was the kind of person who had brothers."

"Well, thank you, all the same, Mr. Swinstead," Temple said hastily and took himself out of the shop.

"Only too degraded, I'm sure," murmured Cecil Swinstead to his departing customer's back.

Temple heard Steve's voice from the sitting room as soon as he entered the flat. She was talking on the telephone and he could tell at once that she was out of her depth. She looked up in relief as he walked into the room.

"Hold on a minute, please. Here he is now."

She clapped a hand over the mouthpiece and stood up to vacate the telephone stool for him.

"Thank God you've come. It's Pasterwake, and he's driving me nearly dotty."

Temple took the receiver and announced himself. He listened in patience for a few minutes, then interrupted firmly.

"Mr. Pasterwake, I appreciate all that you say, but it is quite impossible for me to come and see you this afternoon . . . Yes, quite impossible."

He held the earpiece away and grinned at Steve while another instalment of Pasterwake's monologue came over the wire. When the voice paused Temple said persuasively:

"I can arrange to be free all to-morrow. Then we can discuss the whole problem from beginning to end. Yes, morning and afternoon. At the Dorchester? Very well. Shall we say ten o'clock?"

He put the receiver back and stood up with a satisfied expression.

"Well, Steve, aren't you going to mix me a drink?"

"Paul, what are we doing this afternoon that's so important?"

"We're going to drive down to Seldon Chase and pay a visit to the Honourable George Westeral."

CHAPTER SEVEN

Seldon Chase was a fine Georgian mansion standing in a park of about a hundred acres, some five miles beyond Aylesbury. It was shortly before four when the Frazer Nash rumbled through the old market town; seven minutes later Temple swung in through the gates. Though neither Steve nor he mentioned it, both were thinking that they were now entering the territory of a man whose car had so very nearly ended their lives.

The park was peaceful and typically English under the warm May sunshine, but as they drove up the long avenue Temple noted unmistakable signs of neglect. Westeral had the reputation of being one of the wealthiest young men in London, but it was clear that very little money was available for the upkeep of Seldon Chase. Appearances were kept up to some extent, though, for a butler was waiting for them on the top of an imposing set of steps before the car had come to a halt on the broad sweep of gravel at the front of the house.

"Is his lordship expecting you, sir?" he inquired rather pointedly as Steve and Temple began to mount the steps.

"It was Mr. Westeral we hoped to see. He told me he

would probably be here if we called in. He is at home, I hope?"

"Oh, Mr. Westeral? Yes, sir. If you will come this way— His lordship, you see, is not receiving visitors these days— "

The old man hobbled off ahead of them, mumbling fussily as he went. He parked them in a drawing room which had once been splendid and elegant but was now only a sad reminder of changing times. There were white squares on the walls where pictures had once hung and the tapestry seats of the chairs were faded and worn.

Westeral had heard the car in the drive and appeared almost at once. He did not seem surprised when Temple introduced himself and presented Steve.

"How nice of you to come all this way! Now you're here you'll stay to tea, of course. I'm sorry Jenkie showed you into this mausoleum. I did warn you it was bleak down here, didn't I? Let's go out onto the terrace. I usually have tea out there when I'm here. Are you interested in azaleas, Mrs. Temple? We have a rather good display here. My father won't come down if you don't mind. He really lives in his room all the time now—"

Chatting agreeably he led them through the hall and library, out onto a terrace overlooking the garden. A group of brightly coloured garden chairs, shaded by a Continental umbrella, provided a gay foreground to the sombre and almost derelict background. Glancing up towards the house, Steve was alarmed to see a grey and lined face with frighteningly deep set eyes staring down at her malignantly from behind the curtains of an upstairs window. Thereafter she kept her gaze strictly at ground level, and felt profoundly thankful that Lord Seldon had not joined them for tea.

Westeral was of a type which generally reduced Temple to silence or single-syllable remarks. He was affable and friendly, genuinely solicitous for his guests' comfort and to all appearances really glad to have their company. Temple tried to analyse what it was about him that seemed to make real friendship seem impossible. He decided that Westeral, though charming on the surface, was an only son who had been irretrievably spoilt in his youth and was now completely self-centred.

"I was very glad to hear you had taken this case on, Temple. The police don't seem to be getting anywhere with it. I'm not confident that their methods are always efficacious."

He leaned forward, meeting Temple's eye with what seemed to be complete frankness.

"Now, I don't imagine you've come down here for the sake of my bright eyes. I take it you feel I can help you in some way."

"I think you can," Temple said. "So far I have only a very vague picture of Betty Tyler – and may I say, by the way, that we appreciate how distressing all this is for you."

Westeral acknowledged the remark by dropping his eyes and nodding.

"What I hoped," Temple continued, "is that you would not mind talking about her, giving me an idea of her character and background. I feel there may be some factor there which hasn't come to light yet."

"I don't mind at all," Westeral said. "The police insisted on asking unimaginative questions and gave me no chance to speak out of context at all. The fact of the matter is that I felt there was something about Betty's life which I didn't know. I fell in love with her at first sight, you know, and we became engaged quite quickly. To begin with I found her a perfectly straightforward and natural person."

"Your father didn't object to your engagement in any way?"

"No. On the contrary, he thought it was a good idea for me to marry a sensible girl and settle down. He liked Betty. The fact that she worked for her living made him approve all the more. There was nothing common about Betty, you know."

"Did you ever meet her parents?"

"No, I didn't. Frankly I didn't worry about that. I gathered that there was a mother somewhere who lived in a houseboat and painted pictures. More than that I didn't ask to know."

"I see. What was it about her then that struck you as strange?"

"Well, little things, really. Nothing you could put your finger on. She'd make an appointment to meet me and then either cancel it at the last moment or just leave me standing. This happened quite often and yet she never gave me any explanation. That was what led to our having a row and breaking the whole thing off. I felt that there was some influence in her life that was more important than me and I was not prepared to go on with things unless I knew what it was."

Westeral rose to go to the rescue of Jenkinson, who was wedged in the half-open French windows behind a trolley laden with ancestral tea things. There was enough material in the shape of silverware and china to have stocked a departmental store. Steve, running her eyes over the display, searched in vain for any trace of food. Jenkinson, before his departure, raised the cover of a silver dish and revealed three pieces of buttered toast.

Westeral surveyed the trolley gloomily and then pronounced the sentence she had feared.

"Mrs. Temple, would you be very kind and act as hostess?"

Temple gave her a clandestine wink and turned his attention to Westeral again.

"It was after this row that she had herself transferred to Oxford?"

"Yes. I didn't know anything about it for some time. Meanwhile I'd been telling myself that I hadn't been fair on the girl. That was why I went down to Oxford that day. I hoped I might find that I'd imagined all these difficulties."

"And did you?"

"No." Westeral stared unhappily out over the park. "I felt more than ever that she was dominated by some fear. What made it worse was that she seemed to be in love with me still. It was a miserable lunch. I wanted to stay and take her out to dinner that evening, so as to try and find out what was worrying her, but she said it was impossible and would not even tell me why. I wish I'd insisted on staying on. If I had she might never—"

Westeral bit his lip and broke off. To cover his embarrassment Steve made a great play with the cups and saucers. He made a very quick recovery and was soon on his feet, hunting for sandwiches under the silver covers.

"There's just one more question I want to ask you, Mr. Westeral. Do you remember an occasion about two months ago when Betty was invited down to a house-party here and failed to come?"

Westeral looked blank.

"A house-party here? Such a thing hasn't been known for fifteen years. You see my mother died in 1940 and what with my father's illness—"

"Did she never spend the night here, even?"

Westeral shook his head, obviously puzzled by Temple's query.

"Now forgive me if this sounds a very tactless question. Did you at about that time take Betty Tyler to Paris for the week-end?"

"I'd like to have," Westeral admitted with a smile. "But I knew better than to suggest such a thing to Betty Tyler." He turned towards Steve. "Mrs. Temple, you're very quiet; tell me what you think of the Seldon azaleas."

The conversation drifted away from the Tyler mystery. It was clear that Westeral had said all he wanted to on the subject and Temple did not try to bring it up again.

After tea their host suggested that they might like to walk round the rose garden. It was a thinly disguised pretext to get them on the move. There was little to see in the rose garden but their way back to the front of the house brought them through the courtyard where the garages were. A magnificent Bentley saloon stood out in the open. Temple noticed the Goodwood car park ticket pasted on the windscreen and surmised correctly that this vehicle was the property of son rather than father. Then his eye moved automatically to the number plate. The registration number and initials were exactly the same as those borne by the sports Triumph which they had encountered on the road to Sonning, but no two cars could have been more different.

The Frazer Nash had gone only a hundred yards down the avenue when Steve turned excitedly to Temple.

"You saw what I saw, of course?"

"The registration number of Westeral's car. Yes, I did."

"Someone must have put false number plates on that

Triumph so that if anyone checked up afterwards the car would be traced to Westeral."

"That's a possible explanation," Temple agreed.

"Can you think of another one?"

"As a matter of fact I can."

Steve waited, expecting him to say more but he abruptly changed the subject.

"I was interested by Westeral's suggestions about Betty Tyler's private life. You notice how we never seem to get any nearer to a real picture of her background."

They were outside the gates now. Temple pulled the car into the side of the road and drew a set of road maps out of the pocket.

"What is it, Paul?"

"We're not so very far from Oxford. If we cut back through Thame it's only about twenty five miles." Temple put the maps away and frowned in concentration. "We could be there just about shop-closing time. Now what was the name of that girl Vosper found so helpful?"

"Jill something, I seem to remember."

"Jill Graves. That's it. She seems to have known Betty Tyler pretty well and I've had it in the back of my mind to have a talk with her some time."

As far as timing was concerned they could not have arranged things better. The door of Mariano's Oxford Salon was half closed and the girls were just going home from work. Temple left it to Steve to waylay a smartly dressed brunette who hesitated on the pavement to admire the low, sleek sports car.

"We're looking for Jill Graves," she said. "Can you tell me whether she's gone home yet?"

The girl was instantly on the defensive. She glanced quickly over her shoulder and then walked a little closer to the car. For some odd reason the presence of this expensive piece of machinery seemed to give her confidence in the Temples.

"Are you friends of hers?"

"Well, not exactly. I'm Mrs. Temple and this is my husband."

Temple who had climbed out of the car took off his cap. The girl's eyes had widened with interest.

"Paul Temple? Ooh, I never thought I'd meet you like this. But surely you knew about Jill—"

"Knew what?"

"That she'd disappeared." She bit her words off and glanced again towards the shop. "I suppose it's all right my talking to you like this. Mr. Mariano said we weren't to tell a soul about it—"

"Jill Graves has disappeared. When did this happen?" Temple's voice was sharp and the girl turned back towards him with frightened eyes.

"She hasn't come back to the shop for two days now."

"Have the police been notified?"

"I don't think so. Mr. Mariano said there was no need

to trouble the police. Everything was all right, he said, and there was nothing for anyone to worry about."

For once Steve was alarmed by Temple's driving as they cleared Oxford and took the London road.

"My God!" he muttered. "We should have foreseen this. Betty Tyler, Jane Dallas and now Jill Graves. I should have thought Vosper would have had someone watching her."

"You mean you think she may have been killed too?"

"It doesn't make sense." Temple edged the car through a gap which seemed to leave room for only a motor cyclist and took the speedometer needle up to ninety. "But I don't like the look of it. I wonder what sort of a story Mariano will produce to account for this."

Mariano lived in a flat over his Mayfair premises and his private entrance was through a mauve-painted door opening onto Adam's Row. Temple rang the bell. Almost immediately the door was opened by an automatic device and through a loudspeaker set into the side of the entrance a voice said:

"Please to come up."

They climbed a marble staircase onto which no windows opened but which was lit by concealed lights behind dummy Spanish balconies tumbling with flowers. On the top landing a dark-skinned servant awaited them with an implacable expression.

Temple gave his name and they were shown into a room

which might have been brought stone by stone from the Street of the Flowers in Seville. Mariano was not alone. In the sitting room, which was approached by a flight of steps leading down from the railed landing just inside the doorway, was a very old and stately Spanish lady, and a girl whose looks were surprisingly English.

Mariano came forward to meet the Temples. He was both surprised and delighted to see them.

"You are entering your own home," he said with Spanish courtliness, raising Steve's fingers to his lips. He turned and extended a hand towards the old lady. "This is my mother. I am afraid she speaks no English. And this is someone who has accepted my guardianship for a few days. May I introduce Miss Jill Graves?"

It took the Temples more than a moment to recover from their astonishment. Luckily Mariano was so anxious to account for the situation that he did not notice their discomfiture. The explanation was quite simple. He had seen that Jill Graves was in very much the same situation as Jane Dallas had been and in order to make sure that she came to no harm had brought her as secretly as possible to his own home, under the chaperonage of his mother.

"Mr. Mariano has been very kind," Jill Graves put in. "I really was getting to be quite frightened all by myself in Oxford."

"You knew Betty Tyler very well, I understand."

"Yes. We were real friends."

"You may be able to help me quite a lot, Miss Graves. Would you mind answering some questions for me?"

Mariano was quick to take his cue. He placed his own study at Temple's disposal and left him with the girl. Steve, finding herself alone with the Spaniard and his mother, wondered whether she ought to make small talk in English or try and recall her fading memories of Spanish.

Meanwhile, in response to Temple's prompting, Jill Graves was opening her heart. She was positive, she assured him, that Betty really had been in love with Westeral and was deeply distressed at the breaking of her engagement.

"It has been suggested," Temple said carefully, "that there was some secret influence in her life, something she was apprehensive about. Did you know of anything like that?"

"She was apprehensive, that's exactly the word. I even asked her about it once but she said that she could never tell anyone."

"Did you meet her parents ever?"

For the first time Jill Graves smiled.

"Her mother, yes. Betty took me down to the barge she lives on in Chelsea."

"Why do you smile?"

"Well, she was an extraordinary person to be Betty's mother. Betty was such a lovely person herself but her mother was a real Bohemian. Very masculine and arty – the barge was crammed with pictures she'd painted. But she was devoted to her daughter. Betty told me that she had promised to buy a small shop for her so that she could start her own business. She was only at Mariano's to learn the tricks of the trade."

"Her mother had promised to buy her a business, you say?" In order not to discountenance the girl with a concentrated stare, Temple had found a pencil and was doodling on Mariano's impeccable blotter. "You're sure it was her mother and not her father?"

"I never heard a word spoken about her father. Whether he was dead or they were separated, I don't know."

"Mrs. Tyler made a good deal of money out of her painting, though?"

Jill Graves made a wry face.

"I shouldn't have thought so. I saw a portrait she did once of Betty – it made her look like one of the witches out of Macbeth."

She waited till Temple had stopped laughing before going on.

"Some people must have liked her pictures, though. She even held an exhibition in one of those art galleries in Bond Street."

"Did she now?" Temple leaned forward with interest. "Do you remember the name of the gallery?"

Jill Graves screwed up her eyes and stared at the wall for several seconds before shaking her head.

"I'm afraid I've forgotten the name."

Temple said: "Was it Anderson's Galleries?"

"Yes," the girl nodded emphatically. "That's the name all right."

Temple moved back in his chair with that sense of satisfaction he always felt when what seems like a loose end is neatly tucked back into place. Unaware of the effect of her remark, Jill Graves was chattering on.

"Oddly enough she sold quite a few pictures. I could have sworn half of them had been hung upside down. Betty and I had to laugh about it, though she said to me afterwards: 'Mick's going to be quite above herself after this.' Still, it was nice to see—"

She stopped. Temple had broken the point of Mariano's pencil on his blotter, and was sitting bolt upright.

"Mick? Did you say Mick?"

"Yes. I thought I'd told you. It was a sort of nickname. Everyone called Mrs. Tyler that because she was always dressed like a man. Even Betty used to call her Mick sometimes."

After leaving Mariano's flat, Temple drove straight to Scotland Yard. The constable on duty at the entrance recognised him at once and confirmed that Inspector Vosper was in his office. He must have telephoned the news of the Temples' arrival while the latter were riding up in the lift and tramping along the steely corridor that led to Vosper's room. The Inspector opened his door as soon as he heard their footsteps outside. He was obviously desperately overworked and tired, but he summoned up a smile of welcome as he bowed Steve into his essentially male domain.

"This is an unexpected pleasure. What brings you here at this time of the night? I thought you amateur detectives were always able to avoid work impinging on the sacred hour of dinner."

Temple was accustomed to jibes of this kind from Vosper, especially when the Inspector was strained by overwork.

"If we do like to sit down to meals," he answered without malice, "it's because we have to do all the footwork ourselves. We haven't a large force of hirelings available to do all our dirty work."

Seeing that Vosper was about to launch into a tirade, Steve interrupted quickly.

"We have some interesting news for you, Inspector. We've just come from Mariano's."

"Mariano's?" Vosper sank back into his chair and waved his visitors into a couple of leather-covered easy chairs. "What's he up to now?"

"Well, I think we'd better start at the beginning." Temple tried leaning back in his chair, found it unbearably uncomfortable and sat forward again. "I take it Sir Graham has told you about our trip to Wales?"

Vosper nodded and Temple went on to describe the

visit to Seldon Chase that afternoon. The Inspector tapped the stem of an empty pipe against his teeth as he listened.

"That seems to clear Westeral of complicity in the attempt to kill you. Someone was obviously trying to draw suspicion on to him. What sort of impression did he make on you? Was he worried by your going to see him?"

"He was far from worried," Steve said. "He seemed to be revelling in it. Rather like an actor who has been provided with an unexpected audience. Personally, I thought he could have told us a great deal more about Betty Tyler if he'd cared to."

"Steve was not very smitten by the Honourable George," Temple explained.

"I'm never smitten by anyone who is so completely self-centred and sure of themselves."

"I'm with you there," Vosper agreed. "Which brings us to our second exhibit. What is it with Mariano?"

The Inspector's eyebrows rose when he heard how Mariano had taken Jill Graves under his wing, and when Temple told him that Mrs. Tyler's nickname was Mick he whistled.

"But it must be a coincidence," he objected after a moment's thought. "No woman's going to be mixed up in the murder of her own daughter."

"There are too many coincidences in this case, Inspector. There's a key to it somewhere and I feel that we're not far away from it, now. How have your own inquiries gone?"

The Inspector picked up a bundle of foolscap sheets held together by a vicious bull-dog clip; he turned over half a dozen pages.

"First of all, Shelford. You're sure it was him you saw that night?"

"Quite sure."

"Well, there hasn't been a smell of him since. I wonder if he can have got out of the country again. He must have used some secret escape route after the two murders."

"I believe he's still in the country." Temple spoke quietly but with conviction. "What's more I believe that the night before last was the first time he'd set foot in England for several years."

Vosper's brow furrowed and he shook his head sadly.

"Why are you so persistent in your belief that Shelford is innocent?"

"Before long I hope to be able to answer that question, Inspector. I don't suppose you've been able to find anything on Davis, have you?"

"No. There's too little to go on and Davis may well be an assumed name."

He reached forward and picked up a neatly clipped file from the forward edge of his desk.

"We have a full dossier on Tomlinson, though. Read it through if you want, but there's little to help us. Successful farmer, well liked and respected in the district, gives generously to local charities and all that. Keeps a small string of race horses and hunts throughout the season."

"How long has he been living there?"

"About five and a half years. You can borrow this dossier if you want."

"No, thanks. I'll deny myself that pleasure. Steve, we mustn't take up any more of the Inspector's time."

"Hold on just a moment," the Inspector's voice halted them before they had risen from their seats. "You haven't heard my principal piece of news. Your friend Stephen Brooks is in hospital, after all."

"Oh," Steve glanced towards her husband and saw that he was looking quite crestfallen. "Then it was true about his appendix?"

"No. It's not his appendix that's troubling him. Last night a Soho police patrol found him lying in Bridle Lane. He'd been coshed and razor slashed. If they'd been a quarter of an hour later he'd have bled to death. As it is, his condition is critical."

"Was he able to say who attacked him?"

"He's either unable to speak or too frightened. The doctor would only let me have a few minutes with him. They've had to do a lot of needlework on his face."

Steve shuddered. Brooks had been a good-looking young man, so obviously anxious about whether he was making a favourable or a bad impression on the women he met.

She said: "He has a brother, you remember. Have you notified him?"

"The nearest relation we could find was an aunt," said Vosper, looking at her steadily. "Stephen Brooks has no brother."

Steve swung round to see how Temple had reacted to this piece of information. He appeared quite unmoved, though a line of concentration had appeared between his brows.

"I take it you were able to examine the contents of his pockets. Did you find anything of interest?"

"The usual bits and pieces," Vosper said, pulling open a drawer in his desk, "and this."

He handed Temple a small piece of plain white paper which had been folded in four so that it would fit into a waistcoat pocket. Steve left her chair and came to stand behind her husband as he read the brief inscription on the paper. The writing was unmistakably Brooks' own: 'Crown Jewel 13/5'.

"Good Lord!" Steve breathed. "Don't tell me that all this is a plot to swipe the Imperial State Crown from the Tower of London."

"We needn't go so far as that," Vosper said smugly, "but there are other precious pebbles on the beach."

CHAPTER EIGHT

Temple left the flat in Eaton Square shortly before ten to go out and keep his appointment with Pasterwake. Steve saw him go to the door, kissed him good-bye and wished him good luck.

"What time will you be back, Paul?"

"Oh, about tea time, I expect. What are you going to do with yourself all day?"

"I shall probably go out shopping," Steve said innocently. "Perhaps I'll ring up Mary and meet her for lunch. I'll have tea ready for you when you come back."

"That's a good idea. Try and forget about this Tyler business for a bit."

Steve, however, had other ideas in her head, or rather one very specific idea. She waited only long enough to make sure that her husband was well and truly out of the house before going quickly into her bedroom. She slid the doors of her long wardrobe back and selected the oldest and most casual suit she could find. When she had changed into it and had tied a silk neckerchief over her head she felt less likely to arouse comment on the Chelsea riverside.

She telephoned for a Radio Cab and within three

minutes was climbing in through the door which the cabbie was reaching back to hold open for her.

"Where to, Miss?"

"I'm not sure, really. I want to get to a houseboat that's moored somewhere along the Chelsea embankment." Steve saw the cabbie's look of despair. She added hopefully: "It's called Picasso II."

"Pig what too?"

"Picasso. He's a painter."

"Oh," said the cabbie and put a world of meaning into the word. The handle of his meter went down with a clang. "Well, we'll have a bash at it. Shall we start at Cheyne Walk? That's the respectable end."

Luckily for Steve she had chosen a driver with the patience of Job. After noticing that the first few inquiries yielded no results he made Steve remain in the cab while he trudged into pubs, pulled up alongside delivery vans and hailed road menders knee-deep in square craters. They were all "mate" to the cabbie and seemed to find some convulsing source of amusement in the cabbie's quest for "Picasso II". Steve, reflecting that this was very much a man's world, wondered if there was some sort of club to which you automatically belonged if you hadn't an educated accent. Finally the cabbie drove round to the Post Office and disappeared inside. When he came out his expression was admonitory.

"Naughty. Very naughty."

"What's happened?"

"You told me Chelsea Embankment," the cabbie said gently and very distinctly. "Picasso II is moored on the Battersea Embankment. That's the other side of the river."

"I'm so sorry, Joe," Steve said contritely.

Joe spun the taxi round in the narrow street and headed across Battersea Bridge. Steve wondered why this sort of thing never happened to Paul. It seemed rather unfair.

"Drop me a little distance away, please, Joe," she called through the window.

The taxi turned down a road that led past two tall and gloomy mills and at the end of the wall that enclosed them turned into a small square at the water's edge.

"You're almost there now," the cabbie said. "Just go through the graveyard and you'll find the barges moored to the wall. Cheerful, ain't it?"

The figure on the taximeter was astronomic. Steve added a ten shilling tip and watched the friendly Joe drive away. She felt a little as if she'd been left deserted on a cannibal island. She pushed open the gates that led into St. Mary's Churchyard. The path to the water's edge passed between rows of aged gravestones leaning at eccentric angles. The church itself was empty and closed. When Steve glanced up at the tower the moving clouds gave her the illusion that the building was slowly falling over on her.

There were two barges moored at the wharfs, each

approached by a rickety-looking gangway. Propped against the left-hand one was a rectangular board with the name Picasso II painted on it in crude scarlet letters. The tide was coming in. Water was gurgling between the sides of the barges and the slimy wall, lifting the refuse that had been thrown onto the mud and making the barges stir on their flat bottoms.

Picasso II had once been a Thames sailing barge with lateral keels and tall mast. Now the space once used for storing grain had been converted into living rooms; an improbable structure on the deck housed a flight of steps that led down into the depths. Steve cautiously crossed the gangway and walked along the deck, conscious that the tap of her heels must sound very loud to anyone inside. She rapped on the half open door with her knuckles. From down inside a voice called:

"Whoever it is, come on down. I'm busy."

Steve contemplated the steep flight of steps and wondered whether it was correct to go down backwards or forwards. She decided on the latter and so was able to discover the details of Mrs. Tyler's attire from the feet up – a pair of worn tennis shoes, tight green denim trousers flecked with a hundred different tints of oil paint, a tartan shirt with sleeves rolled up to the elbow. Mrs. Tyler was squat and robust. Although in certain ways unmistakably feminine, she had cut her hair as short as a man's, perhaps to match her deep, rather gruff voice. She was standing in front of an easel, dabbing at a painting that was a blaze of vivid colour. Though she found it impossible to tell what the subject was, Steve found herself fascinated by its brilliance and power. Mrs. Tyler added a stroke of Veridian Tint before pushing her brush into a jar of turpentine and turning to direct a penetrating stare at Steve.

"I hope you'll forgive my coming like this, Mrs. Tyler—"

"You seem to know my name. What's yours?"

Steve was not unprepared for this question but its suddenness put her off balance for a moment.

"I'm Lucille Draper," she said, using the first name that came into her head. "I saw your exhibition at the Anderson Galleries and I was very attracted by your work."

"Oh, yes?"

Mick Tyler had turned away and was wiping her paint-stained hands on a rag. To judge by the appearance of her fingers she used them more than her brushes to get the paint onto the canvas.

"I've been meaning for some time to have my portrait done," Steve went on, trying to ignore the dangerous frown that was gathering on the other woman's forehead. "I want to give it to my husband as a surprise for his birthday—"

"Your husband?"

She turned towards Steve as if astonished at the idea that any woman should want to present herself to a man as seen through the eyes of Mick Tyler.

"I'm not a photographer, you know. If I paint you it'll

have to be as I see you. He may not like it very much."

"I'll take a chance on that," Steve said with a smile. "He's got plenty of photographs of me anyway."

"Turn your head a little."

Mick was suddenly viewing Steve's head with a professional eye. She turned her head obediently. Out of the corner of her eye she could see her hostess dodging about, now stooping, now standing on tip-toe.

"I'd like to do you," she said suddenly. "I think I know how I can do it. Only I mustn't lose this impression. Do you mind sitting in that chair and keeping your expression just like that?"

She manœuvred Steve into a surprisingly comfortable easy chair, then seized a drawing block and a chunk of charcoal.

"Lean your head back. I want you perfectly relaxed."

Steve obeyed and for three minutes Mick drew with absorption. Although she had come in order to talk Steve knew it would be fatal to try and break through Mick's concentration. At the end of that time the artist put down her block and pencil.

"Either I get it at once or not at all," she said. "I'd like to take this a stage further this morning, if you don't mind. Have you an hour or so to spare?"

"Of course," Steve said. "It's very good of you to start so promptly."

"I'm like that. When I've made up my mind to do a

thing I do it. Now, I suggest we have a cup of coffee first and then we can settle down to work."

She disappeared through a doorway and presently there came the pop of a gas ring being lit. Left alone Steve glanced round the room. The place was in picturesque disorder. Painting accessories, half finished canvases, articles of clothing and eating utensils lay about in amicable confusion. There were no windows in the sides of the barge and the only light came through the skylights on the deck. It was terribly hot and stuffy under the water-tight deck. Mick was not the sort of person to encourage fresh air.

She came back with two cups of coffee and set one down beside Steve. A half empty bottle of Jamaica rum stood on a low table. Mick uncorked it and poured a liberal dose into her own cup. She glanced inquiringly at Steve.

"For you?"

"No, thank you."

"I always think a little something in one's coffee is a good idea."

Now that the first passion of creation had been expended, Mick was able to work more composedly on her sketch and to Steve's relief she seemed prepared to talk.

"Smoke if you want to," Mick said when her visitor had finished her coffee. "I want you to feel relaxed."

They talked about general topics for a while and touched very briefly on politics. Mick's views on the subject of politicians were simple and anarchistic.

"I'd put the whole lot up against the wall and shoot them."

"It's rather curious that I should be sitting here talking to you like this," Steve said, daring at last to raise the subject which had brought her here. "I once had my hair dressed by your daughter. She was such a charming girl. It must have been a terrible loss to you."

At first she thought that Mick had not heard. She glanced round and saw her sitting as motionless as a piece of granite, her eyes staring through the sides of the barge.

"Yes," she said at last. "A terrible loss." Her eyes swung back to Steve and the expression in them was frightening.

" 'Vengeance is mine. I will repay, saith the Lord'."

The Biblical quotation coming from Mrs. Tyler was startling. Steve started to say something conventional, but her voice was drowned by the other woman's resonant tones.

"But here on earth too there will be retribution. You will see. It shall not go unpunished."

All of a sudden Steve wished she had not come. It was painful to witness this exposure of human emotions and she knew she could not bring herself to question Mick Tyler further. The air in the barge was becoming thick and oppressive. She could feel her temples throbbing. The other woman's voice seemed to be fading away into the distance. She made an effort to pull herself together.

"Mrs. Tyler, I wonder if you'd mind opening a window. I'm afraid I'm feeling rather dizzy."

"It is close in here. But I'm sorry to say that none of these windows open."

She rose and came to the side of Steve's chair. Steve tried to sit up but Mick put a hand on her forehead and gently pressed her back.

"You'll feel all right in a moment. Just let yourself relax. I'll go and fetch you a glass of water, shall I?"

Steve had experienced the sensations which follow an overdose of alcohol, but she had never before known this odd feeling; a black sea was rising around her, taking the weight out of her limbs, inviting her to surrender consciousness and float away on its gentle waves. She made a last attempt to sit upright, came to the conclusion that it wasn't worth the effort and let her head fall back on the cushion.

She was completely unconscious when Mick came back from the kitchen. Mick looked at the bottle of tablets in her hand and smiled ruefully.

"I wish they'd send me to sleep as quickly as that."

It was already past tea time when Temple returned from his discussions with Pasterwake. Negotiations had begun stormily but in the end everything had been settled much more satisfactorily than he had dared to hope. He came into the flat bursting to tell Steve his news and felt curiously deflated when he found she was not there. It was a rare thing for Steve to break her word and she had said she would have tea waiting for him. He warned himself not to be fussy and went into the study to do some work and fill in the time of waiting.

After an hour the continued silence of the flat began to be ominous. He pulled the telephone towards him and dialled Mary Larrington's number. Steve, she told him, had not so much as rung up to suggest lunching together. He rang for Charlie and went out to meet him in the hall as he came through from his own room.

"Charlie, what time did Mrs. Temple go out this morning?"

"Very shortly after you, sir. About ten-thirty I should think."

"And she hasn't been back since?"

"No."

"She didn't ring up with any message?"

Charlie shook his head. "That's a funny thing too," he said sucking his teeth reflectively, "because she told me she'd be here in good time for tea. She was going to buy some cakes at that French shop."

Temple went down the stairs and walked quickly round to the garage where he kept his car. The Frazer Nash was in its usual place and the garage attendant had not seen anything of Steve all day.

"Are you wanting the car now, sir?"

"Yes," Temple said. "Now that I'm here I'll take her round to the flat."

He was beginning to feel seriously worried about Steve. He knew her well enough to realise that she had her teeth well into the Tyler mystery. She was quite capable of trying to surprise him with some sensational new discovery on his return from the Dorchester. He wished now that he had warned her not to play with fire. The suspicion which had taken him round to the garage was that she had driven down to Seldon Chase to try and charm some more information out of George Westeral. Since the car was still in the garage it was likely that she was somewhere in Town. He saw now that it was much more probable that she had decided to follow up the suggestion that Betty Tyler's mother was the Mick referred to by Davis and Tomlinson. Steve would naturally feel that this feminine angle was one with which she was best equipped to deal.

He ran up to the flat for long enough to telephone his friend Superintendent Herbert of the Thames Police.

"It's Temple here. I wonder if you can help me with a piece of information. Do you know the whereabouts of a houseboat called Picasso II, moored somewhere along the Chelsea reach?"

"Hold on just a minute. We should be able to answer that one."

He was back in less than two minutes with the answer to Temple's query.

"Picasso II is moored at the wall just beside St. Mary's Church. That's on the Battersea side, north of Battersea bridge. She's a converted sailing barge. Do you want us to take a look at her?"

"No," Temple said emphatically. "For heaven's sake keep well away. Thanks for the information."

He warned Charlie to stay near the telephone, almost broke his neck getting down the stairs four at a time and slipped the Frazer Nash out into the thickening rush hour traffic. The speedometer needle pointed to sixty more often than thirty as he threaded his way along the Embankment using the car's brakes and acceleration to the full. He crossed Battersea Bridge and finally stopped at almost the exact spot where Joe had dropped Steve six hours earlier.

The sun was sinking fast; gravestones cast long shadows over the path as he walked through the churchyard, his eyes alert for any movement on Picasso II. He could hear dishes clattering in the galley as he crossed the gangway. The noise stopped abruptly when his feet sounded on the deck and he could imagine unseen ears listening for the rap of his knuckles on the door.

"Come on in," a deep voice called. Temple could not be sure whether it was a man's or a woman's.

He clambered down the steps and was confronted by Mick Tyler as she emerged from her small kitchen. Her hands and forearms glistened with greasy washing up water and a half-smoked cigarette dangled from her lips. After one glance Temple understood why she had a masculine nickname.

"Mrs. Tyler?"

She nodded.

"My name is Temple. Has my wife paid you a visit to-day?"

He had decided that his best course was to go straight to the point. As Vosper had said, it was impossible to believe that the mother of Betty Tyler could be implicated in her murder.

"Your wife? Why on earth should she want to visit me?"

"You may perhaps have read that I am assisting the police in their inquiries about the death of your daughter I have good reason to believe she came here to see you. She has not returned home and has not been seen since."

Temple put as much authority and emphasis into his words as he could, but so far from being shaken Mick seemed fortified by what she heard.

"I've never set eyes on your wife and what's more I don't much care for your tone of voice."

"I'm sorry," Temple said more quietly. "You can understand that I am naturally perturbed at her failure to show up. It is possible that she did not give you her real name."

Temple was allowing his eyes to rove round the untidy

room as he spoke. He hoped that he might find some sign that Steve had been here, but apart from an ash tray which bore a half-smoked cigarette stained with lipstick there was no trace of any female visitor.

"No one's been to see me to-day. If your wife had come asking questions I can assure you I'd very quickly have shown her the door. I'm just about fed up with all the questions they've been asking and all to no purpose. The murderer of my Betty is still walking round as free as you and me."

Her manner was defiant and Temple decided that there was nothing to be gained in pressing her further. He left her, half convinced that she was telling the truth, and climbed up the stairs again into the comparatively clean air of the Thames. As he crossed the gangway he paused. Mick, like other dwellers on the river, was in the habit of dumping her rubbish and trusting to the outgoing tide to take it away. A trick of the current had collected the contents of her wastepaper basket and deposited them in a cranny just under the gangway. It was one of these scraps of paper which had caught his eye. From the galley down below the sound of protesting china proclaimed that Mick had renewed her assault on the washing up. Temple knelt and with one hand on the rail, leant down to fish the scrap of paper from the cranny. He stuffed it in his pocket and went back to his car. Once there he laid the moist piece of paper on the passenger's seat. The sheet had been torn in four and the charcoal outlines were blurred but even from the quarter he had rescued he had no difficulty in recognising Steve's cheekbone, eye and hair.

Without being quite conscious of what he was doing he started the car up and engaged a gear. The sight of Steve's features so vividly portrayed on that mangled piece of paper had shaken him badly but some instinct warned him that he must go on behaving normally. Mick Tyler could still be peering out at him from some peep-hole on Picasso II. She must believe that he had swallowed what she had told him.

But she had been lying. Steve had been to the house-boat, was perhaps still there, battened somewhere out of sight under the decks.

Temple drove on down the street a little way. It was a deserted part of the waterfront and apart from a delivery van and newsboy going his rounds with the evening papers there was nobody about. He struggled to recover his power to think coolly and rationally. Now, just when he needed them most, his faculties were deserting him. This was so close, so personal a danger. He dared not let his mind dwell too long on what might have happened to Steve. The thought of the black, muscular water he had seen feeling its way round the sides of Picasso II was like a drug, numbing his brain.

He supposed that the sensible thing to do was notify Scotland Yard or telephone the friendly Superintendent

Herbert. But he was determined not to act hurriedly. Steve's safety was now what counted most with him, and he was not confident that the intervention of the police was what would help her most.

He found an alleyway in which to turn the car and was reversing into it when his attention was arrested by a small figure standing at the entrance to the public house on the corner. He was watching the car intently, but as soon as Temple looked towards him he spun round and dived into the Public Bar.

"Badger!" Temple said to himself. "Now I wonder what mischief brings him here."

Badger was one of his many underworld informants. On several occasions Badger had given him useful tips and in return Temple had persuaded the police to drop certain minor charges against him. Acting partly on a hunch and partly on the need for a drink, Temple reversed right back and parked the car unobtrusively behind the "Star and Garter".

Badger, true to the name by which he was known to both criminals and police, was hunched in a corner of the bar nibbling a glass of beer and trying to look inconspicuous. Temple ordered a whisky for himself and took it to the table where the little crook was sitting.

"All right, Badger. You know it's no good trying to hide from me. What's on your conscience this time?"

Reluctantly Badger came out of his shell. He affirmed,

in his own special jargon, that his soul was as white as snow and his record since Temple had last seen him as clean as a Chelsea Pensioner's Income Tax Form.

"Splendid," Temple told him. "Then you won't mind answering one or two questions for me. The Battersea river front is your speciality isn't it? Tell me, do you know the owner of a houseboat called Picasso II? Her name is Mrs. Tyler – more generally known as Mick Tyler."

Badger glanced towards the barman whose ears were twitching with the effort to try and overhear the conversation between Badger and this well-dressed gentleman who was so unlike the usual brand of customer seen in the "Star and Garter".

"What's in this for me?" Badger inquired hoarsely.

"That depends on what you can do for me. Have you ever known me let you down?"

Badger took a gulp of beer and wiped his mouth with the back of his hand. He hadn't shaved that day and the length of ropey cloth tied round his neck seemed to have been in position for a good month. He exuded a faint aroma reminiscent of barrels, tar and dog kennels. Temple felt for a cigarette and lit up.

"I didn't know Mick was crook," Badger said. "I wouldn't have touched it if I had."

"Oh? So you do know her, then?"

"Who doesn't? Some of them think she's crazy enough to be locked up, but I'm not so sure – I think she has her head screwed on all right. Some of these arty folk is like that naturally."

"You'll have another one, Badger?"

Temple was suddenly elated. Following Badger into the "Star and Garter" had been a forlorn hope and now the little man had plunged straight into the heart of the matter with practically no prompting. Perhaps he had learnt from past experience that when trouble loomed up it paid to be on the same side as Temple.

"Thanks, I will," he said, and added quickly, "Whisky, same as you're having."

"Now then," Temple went on when the drink had been brought. "How do you come to know so much about Mick Tyler?"

"Well, see, it's usually me that takes the messages to her from Fred."

"Messages?"

"Yes. She hasn't got no telephone on that barge and Fred lets her have her messages sent here. Then I usually takes them over when I comes on duty at opening time like."

"She receives a good many messages?"

"There's usually two or three every day. Has been lately at any rate."

"Have you any idea who these messages are from or what they're about?"

Badger's expression became one of injured professional

pride. He drank some of his whisky and looked at Temple over the side of the glass.

"You don't believe as I'd read other people's letters, Mr. Temple?"

His eyes never left Temple's left hand as it moved to the pocket where his wallet was kept.

"I'm sure you wouldn't stoop so low, Badger. But unless they were put in sealed envelopes you might, quite by accident, have noticed a signature or a name."

His hand had been withdrawn from the pocket, bringing with it a leather-backed notebook. He selected a blank page and wrote a list of names on it.

"I want you to read this list, Badger, and tell me if any of the messages have been signed with one of these names."

Badger drew the list towards him and bowed his head till his eyes were a few inches from the paper. His lips moved as his finger grubbed down the list.

"Davis," he said presently and turned back to Temple. "That's the name that was on most of the messages."

"Good." Temple took his notebook back and felt for a pencil. "How would you like to earn a tenner?"

Badger licked his lips. The question did not in his opinion need an answer. Temple tore a page out of his book and scribbled a message on it.

"Has Mick Tyler a car?" he asked as he folded the paper. Badger nodded, his eyes avid. "Where does she keep it?"

"Round at Blundell's Garage. It's about a hundred yards

the other side of the houseboat. She runs one of them new Morrises."

Temple folded the message in half and handed it over. Then he took out his wallet and extracted a five pound note, which he also gave to Badger.

"Now, Badger. I want you to take this note to Mick Tyler. You can take your time about it. Tell her it came in the usual way. When you get back here there'll be another fiver waiting for you."

Badger finished up his drink and sidled out of the pub. When he had gone Temple stood up and moved over to the bar counter.

"You must be Fred," he said to the proprietor, a fat jolly man who was polishing the top of the bar counter with a damp cloth.

"That's me."

"I wonder if you'd be kind enough to let me have an envelope?"

Fred was very glad to oblige. Temple took the envelope sealed another five pound note inside it and asked Fred to hand it to Badger as soon as he returned.

"By the way," Temple said as he turned away. "Do you know Mick Tyler at all well?"

"I know most of the people round here," Fred said noncommittally.

"What's happened to her husband these days? I haven't seen him for a long time."

"Archie? No, he's stopped coming any more." The barman chuckled at some amusing memory. "Reckon he realised at last he was boxing in the wrong weight."

"What's he doing with himself now?"

"I did hear he'd started a book-making business somewhere up in the North. That would be just his line. I can imagine the little chap standing on a barrel, doing all this sort of thing."

Fred gave a vivid imitation of the gestures of a tic-tac man and they both laughed.

"Don't worry," the barman called as Temple went out. "I'll give this to old Badger."

Temple had no difficulty in locating Blundell's garage. He parked his car nearby and began to walk carefully towards Picasso II. He was just in time to see Badger emerge from the churchyard gates and scuttle back towards the "Star and Garter" as fast as his legs would carry him.

It was beginning to grow dark. He found an abandoned house whose nailed-up doorway offered him a refuge from which he could observe the gates of the churchyard. He only had to wait five minutes before Mick appeared. She was in a hurry and was moving rather wildly. But she had tied a muffler round her head and was trying to stuff her arms down the sleeves of an old raincoat. She closed the churchyard gates and turned towards Blundell's garage.

Temple, at the wheel of the Frazer Nash, was ready and waiting when the black Morris saloon bounced out of the garage. He made a note of the number and pulled out to follow Mick as she pointed the nose of the car southward.

It was not difficult to keep the tail of the Morris in view as it moved up Battersea Bridge Road and then swung left towards Nine Elms Lane. Mick was not the kind of driver who pays much regard to the traffic behind her and it never occurred to her to check whether she was being followed. Occasionally she cut viciously in front of other cars and Temple dropped a few places, but with his superior manoeuvrability he was always able to catch up again. She led him along the Albert Embankment, past the old Festival of Britain site and into Southwark Street. Luckily it was almost dark by then and he was able to close right up on her. Otherwise he might have missed her when she abruptly turned off the main thoroughfare and plunged into the maze of streets that led down to the water's edge.

They entered a domain of high walls, warehouses and bombed sites which Temple had never explored before. Mick must have come this way often for she swung the Morris to left and to right without hesitation. Eventually she pulled off the street on to a square which had been flattened in 1941 and never built up again. She switched off her engine and climbed out.

Temple turned his lights off and parked his own car in the shadow of a wall. This was an area of London's dockland which was quite deserted after working hours. Overhead the sky was lit by the orange glow of the city.

Just across the Thames the Tower loomed up weirdly against the lights of modern London. The confused murmur of traffic formed a background to closer sounds – the shouts of children playing in a nearby street, the blast of a tug's hooter on the river. Making no noise in his rubber-soled shoes, Temple followed Mick down a narrow alley that led like a chasm between two tall warehouses. When he emerged at the far end he almost bumped into Mick. She was standing in the pool of light cast by an old-fashioned gas lamp, peering anxiously up and down the street. Temple drew back into the shadows and watched her. His hope that she might lead him straight to Steve was beginning to fade. It was obvious that she was intending to wait here until someone turned up.

He gave it five minutes and then walked silently towards her till he was standing a yard behind her shoulder.

"Mick!"

She spun round at the unexpected voice, saw Temple and stepped quickly back a couple of paces.

"What are you doing here?"

"Where is she, Mrs. Tyler?"

"I don't know what you're talking about. I suppose you think you're clever, following me down here." She had recovered very quickly from her surprise and fallen back for her defence on the old blustering manner. "I've come to meet a friend; he'll know how to take care of you when he arrives."

She was glancing up the street as she spoke, hoping to see some less hostile figure materialising out of the gloom.

"Your friend isn't coming, Mrs. Tyler. Hadn't you better start telling me the truth? Where is my wife?"

"I've told you already, I don't know anything—"

"Just a minute," Temple cut in. "Badger brought you a message this evening, didn't he?"

Mick Tyler glanced sharply at him but didn't answer.

"Shall I tell you what was in that message? It said: 'Serious development concerning Steve T. Imperative I see you. Come at once to the usual place. Davis'."

Temple allowed her a moment to digest the implications of these words. Then he said quietly:

"If you knew nothing about the disappearance of Steve Temple you would have ignored that message or at least handed it over to the police. But you weren't surprised. You were accustomed to receiving messages from Davis and having Badger deliver them. What's more you knew perfectly well what had happened to Steve—"

Mick's move was so swift that it took Temple unawares. She punched her fist into his stomach and ran for the opening of the alleyway with surprising speed. She was halfway along it before he caught up with her. This time he took her arm in a grip which she could not break.

"You just listen to me," he said between clenched teeth. "Two girls have been brutally murdered and now my own wife is missing. I don't know what your part in it is, but do you think I'd hesitate to wring your neck if I thought it would bring me nearer to her? Now tell me the truth or I swear I'll march you into the nearest police station."

Mick Tyler had had enough and she was gasping from the pain caused by Temple's ferocious grip on her arm.

"They've got her at the warehouse," she whispered. "I don't know how you reach it from here, but you can tell by the sign. It's called Burgess Cork and Timber Shippers."

"Is Steve alive?"

"She was when I saw her last."

"How long ago was that?"

"About three o'clock, I should say."

"Could you take me to this warehouse? It won't pay you to try and hide anything from me now."

"I only know how to reach it by river. It's somewhere near here."

Mick was sullen but he was sure that she was at last telling him the truth.

"Burgess Cork and Timber Shippers."

Knowing that he was close to Steve now gave him a feeling of almost unbearable urgency. He was still reluctant to call on the police. His instinct was to get to Steve's side and be with her in whatever danger she faced. The problem was what to do with Mick while he set about locating the warehouse.

"You'd better get in that car and drive back to your barge," he said. "And I advise you not to start sending any messages. If I find Steve unhurt you may just get away with it. But otherwise – God help you!"

Mick Tyler seemed eager enough to take the hint. He saw her back to the car and watched her drive out of the small square. He wondered if he were making a fatal mistake.

The steady light of a telephone kiosk seemed to be the one friendly feature in this alien world. He walked across to it and saw with annoyance that the directories had been stolen, so that the method of locating the warehouse was barred to him.

He was about to allow the door to swing shut when a thought struck him. It would be a wise precaution to inform Charlie of what he was intending to do. If after an hour there was no message from him, Charlie could notify Sir Graham.

He felt for the pennies in his trousers pocket, inserted them in the slot and dialled his own number. He could hear the regular buzz-buzz as the bell rang in the flat and he pictured Charlie hurrying through from his own quarters. He made a mental note to have an extension installed in Charlie's room. The receiver was lifted before the expected time had elapsed.

"Hullo. Who is it?"

Temple stood, unable to believe his ears, so astounded that he forgot to press Button A.

"Who is it?" the voice repeated. It sounded terribly tired

and sleepy as if its owner could barely make the effort to keep awake.

Temple at last recovered the use of his limbs. The coins clattered down into the box as he pressed the button. A curious lump had come up into his throat so that he could only say one word.

"Steve!"

CHAPTER NINE

Doctor Hitchcock closed the door of Steve's bedroom and walked with deliberation back into the sitting room. Sir Graham Forbes and Temple were standing in the centre of the room close to the trolley of food which Charlie had brought in to satisfy his master's needs. Temple was absent-mindedly munching chicken and egg sandwiches while Sir Graham browsed over a whisky and soda and watched him in silence.

"Nothing whatsoever to worry about," Doctor Hitchcock said. He nodded assent as Temple laid a hand invitingly on the whisky decanter. "She has had an abnormally heavy dose of one of the less common sleeping draughts. I should think it must have been prescribed for someone in a very advanced state of nervous exhaustion."

"That makes sense," Temple murmured. "How long is she going to be like this, John? I couldn't get a word of sense out of her when I came in."

"In the ordinary course of events," Hitchcock said judiciously, "I should have preferred to let her sleep it off quite naturally, but in view of what you told me I gave her something that should wake her up a little. It'll require a few minutes to take effect. When she does go to sleep again it will be for a long time. I advise allowing her to rest as long as she wants."

The doctor saw that Sir Graham was fretting for him to take himself away. He broke into the polite small talk which Temple was trying to keep going, pleaded that he had another call to answer and went on his way. Temple was just returning from seeing him to the front door when Steve emerged from her bedroom, knotting the sash of a silk dressing gown round her waist. She was a little pale and rather tousled, but her eyes were wide open. He took her in his arms and they stood for a few moments.

"Oh, Steve," he whispered. "Why do you do these things to me?"

"Darling Paul. You're really glad to see me again, aren't you?"

"Sir Graham is here, champing to know what this is all about. Do you feel like talking? I must confess I'm rather curious myself."

"Oddly enough, I feel marvellous; just as if I'd had a bottle of champagne. I expect the hangover will hit me later!"

Sir Graham was very courtly and solicitous for Steve's well-being. He settled her in a deep arm chair and padded her round with cushions. Steve had to suppress a sudden desire to weep when she saw him kneel to place a stool under her feet.

"I must do this more often," she said with forced gaiety. "I like being made a fuss of."

"Now, Steve." Temple sat on the floor with his back to the side of the fireplace. "Let's have it. I gather you took it into your head to go visiting this morning. Mrs. Tyler gave you a pretty warm reception?"

She nodded ruefully and went on to tell them of everything that had passed between her and Mick Tyler until the moment when she had lost consciousness.

"I think I must have been taken down the river by boat. I have vague memories of waves and the dark shadows of bridges passing overhead. But I have no recollection of being taken ashore. Someone splashing cold water in my face woke me up – hours later it seemed. I found I was lying on straw in that warehouse place. Mick Tyler had vanished. There was only a strange man I've never seen before and the person you and I saw at Crow's Farm, Paul."

"Davis."

"Yes. The other man used that name, I remember now."

Sir Graham put his oar in quietly. "Did you get the other's name – the one you hadn't seen before?"

"No. Davis called him Fred but that was all."

"Go on, Steve. They tried to make you talk, I suppose."

Steve's brows puckered as she wondered whether she was remembering everything correctly. She had noticed the hard edge on Temple's voice and knew what he was expecting to hear.

"They weren't tough with me at all, Paul. Davis seemed to know who I was – "

"Why is that so surprising? Didn't you tell Mick—?"

"No. I said I was Mrs. Lucille Draper."

"But Steve!" Temple protested. "Why on earth use that name?"

"She asked me rather suddenly. It was the first name I thought of. It seemed better than trying to dream up some bogus name like Matilda Bogglesworthy."

"So Davis was all smiles and condolences, was he?"

"No, he wasn't smiling, Paul dear," Steve said rather tartly. "But there was nothing – physical. He seemed to know we had been down to Crows Farm and tried to find out how much we'd seen. I didn't tell him anything. Then there followed rather an odd bit of conversation. He suddenly said something like: 'Your husband is making an awful fool of himself. He'll never pin these murders on Harry Shelford.' I was stung into answering without thinking. I said: 'On the contrary, he's quite certain that Shelford had nothing to do with them.' Davis was completely silenced. Somehow I seemed to have taken all the wind out of his sails. He disappeared for quite a long time after that. I don't know how long it was because all I wanted was to go to sleep. They woke me up with cold water again and Davis made me stand up. He said: 'You're a very lucky girl. We're going to let you go this time. But give Temple this message: he'd better keep out of this or he'll do more harm than good. Justice will take its course without his intervention.' It was something like that anyway, Paul."

"Here comes Vosper," Sir Graham said.

Temple scrambled to his feet and laid his hand for a second on Steve's as he went to meet the Inspector. Charlie had hurried to answer his ring at the bell and now ushered him into the room. There was an unusually sharp nip in the air for a May night. Vosper was rubbing his hands and his cheeks were pink.

"Come on, Inspector, and get something warm inside you. There are plenty of sandwiches here if you're hungry."

"Business first, Mr. Temple, thank you. Glad to see you're none the worse, Mrs. Temple." He turned towards Sir Graham and his smile included the whole room.

"Bit better here than at the Yard, eh sir? That's why I like to have Mr. Temple in on the job. Detection de luxe, home comforts laid on."

"You can cut out the poetics, Inspector," remarked Sir Graham. "What have you to report?"

Vosper quickly clamped his official expression onto his face.

"I made contact with the River Police, sir, and we had no difficulty in locating Burgess's warehouse. We made a thorough search of the premises."

"Any results?"

"All we ascertained was that whatever the Burgess company used to ship it was not cork and timber."

"What is it, then?" Temple asked sharply.

"That's hard to say, sir. The analysts will be able to tell us. But we found leaves that looked suspiciously like tobacco."

"Have you had time to check up on this Burgess company Vosper?"

The Inspector met his chief's eye with a certain complacency.

"I have, sir. They went out of business eighteen months ago."

He waited to see whether Sir Graham would express any surprise at the speed with which he had unearthed this information. Then, since no comment was forthcoming, he went on:

"I then proceeded up river to the barge Picasso II, where I interviewed Mrs. Tyler. I cautioned her and then asked her to tell me what her movements had been to-day. She adopted a very hostile and offensive manner. She admitted that a lady visited her this morning but stated that she gave her name as Mrs. Draper."

Steve moved a little uncomfortably among her cushions.

"She denies administering any form of drug and produced the theory that her visitor had been drinking. She affirms that Mrs. Draper left her at about mid-day, very unsteady on her feet."

"Mick will have to do better than that," Temple said.

"Indeed she will," agreed Sir Graham briskly. "I think

we have grounds for making an arrest, Inspector. You'd better equip yourself with a warrant—"

Temple put his glass down and stepped forward.

"Sir Graham, I wonder if I could make a request of you?"

"What is it, Temple?"

"Don't arrest Mick Tyler just yet."

Sir Graham stared at Vosper. The Inspector looked down at his notebook.

"But damn it!" Sir Graham exploded. "The woman was responsible for kidnapping your wife."

"I know. I'm almost certain that it was a mistake, though. Mick Tyler may not have known that Steve was my wife but I think she did know that she was not Lucille Draper. I don't honestly believe we have anything to fear from her. In fact, it is she who is in danger of her life."

There was a moment's silence. Then Sir Graham said: "Would you care to elaborate that remark, Temple?"

"Not just at this moment, Sir Graham. But I would most earnestly recommend you to put a plain clothes man to watch Picasso II."

Sir Graham walked to the far corner of the room. His back was turned to them all while he stooped to survey some porcelain ornaments in a small cupboard.

"We seem to reach this point in a good many cases, Temple. I won't say that you haven't been often right in the past. But it is now well over a week since Betty Tyler was killed and we have three unsolved murders on our hands."

"Three?"

Sir Graham turned round deliberately and gave Temple the full force of his very authoritative gaze.

"Stephen Brooks died in hospital this afternoon."

Steve caught her breath. Vosper moved quietly to the trolley and helped himself to a couple of sandwiches. Temple took the stopper out of the decanter and poured himself a small measure of whisky. In the hall outside the baby grandfather clock softly chimed the twelve strokes of midnight.

"So you see," Sir Graham said after the long pause, "we cannot afford to take any liberties. We simply must show some results soon."

"To-day is Friday, isn't it?"

"Thursday," Sir Graham said, then caught Vosper's movement and corrected himself. "Well, I suppose it's early on Friday morning."

"If I told you that you will know the person responsible for these murders the day after to-morrow would you be satisfied?"

"I'd be very satisfied if I was confident of it. Am I to presume that you know who it is already?"

"I don't know," Temple said, placing special emphasis on the last word. "And I'm afraid I have another request to make of you. Would it be possible to find some pretext to search Tomlinson's place?"

"At Davidstown?"

"Yes."

"Quite impossible, I'm afraid, Temple. We should need a warrant and at this moment I have no justification for asking for one – unless there is some information which you are withholding from me."

"I'm not withholding anything – except perhaps vague ideas. You've had all the information I've had and a good deal more besides."

Steve sensed that the discussion was beginning to go in the wrong direction. She alone realised the strain which that day's events had imposed on her husband, but she saw at the same time that Sir Graham was deeply troubled and felt his responsibility weighing heavily on his shoulders. She stood up and faced the men.

"I'm afraid I'm beginning to feel terribly wobbly. Paul, would you mind giving me a hand? You will excuse him for a moment, Sir Graham?"

Sir Graham was instantly contrite.

"Steve, how unforgivable of us to use your drawing room as our office. We're on our way at once. Come on Vosper."

He turned at the door and sent an anxious glance back at Temple.

"You'll keep in touch, won't you, Temple?"

Both the Temples sighed with relief when the front door thudded and they knew they were alone together.

"It's really you who ought to be tired, Paul. I've been asleep nearly all day. That man Davis was really quite nice to me. I didn't have time to tell you but he put me in a taxi and paid the fare to Eaton Square. I don't think he's a really criminal type."

"Now listen, Steve." Temple placed his hands on Steve's shoulders and made her face him. "Mr. Davis is somehow mixed up in a racket which has cost three people their lives. You've got to be more careful. There must be no more private investigations by Mrs. Temple."

Steve pouted and dropped her eyes.

"I'm serious, Steve. We're coming to the phase which is always tricky. As we come closer and closer to the murderer we become more and more personally involved – not just me but both of us. So please take what I say seriously."

He took his hands from Steve's shoulders and went to the windows to fasten the catches and switch on the burglar alarms. Then he moved out to the hall door and shot the two heavy bolts that reinforced the mortice lock. Just to be on the safe side he went round the whole flat, checking the locks and window catches. By the time he had put on his pyjamas and walked through from his dressing room to the bedroom Steve was fast asleep.

*

Steve woke slowly from her very deep sleep to find that her room was full of sunlight and the bed beside her empty. She stared at her bedside clock, unable to believe that it was already mid-day. Charlie came promptly in answer to her ring wearing that smug expression which early risers inflict on those who lie late in bed.

"Where's the master, Charlie?"

"He went out, oh, about nine o'clock."

"Did he leave any message?"

"He said he expected to be back for lunch and you weren't to worry. Shall you have your breakfast now? I have a tray all ready for you."

Steve yawned and stretched her arms.

"I'll just have orange juice, thank you, Charlie. It's very nearly lunch time, isn't it?"

She drank the orange juice and went into her bathroom to turn the taps on. While she was luxuriating in the warm water she heard the telephone ringing and Charlie hurrying to answer it. He was hardly back in the kitchen again when it rang once more. She heard his voice murmuring in the sitting room as he placated some impatient caller.

"Who was it?" she called through the door, as she heard Charlie's footsteps returning.

"That Pastrycook, or whatever his name is. He can't seem to understand that Mr. Temple has other things to do besides sign film contracts."

"And before that?"

"Some funny character who thought he could make me laugh by telling me his name was Mary Ann."

"Poor Mariano," Steve murmured.

"Of course, Sir Graham's been on a couple of times. What's wrong with him these days? He's like a bear with a sore head."

Steve was dressed in time to greet her husband with a cocktail when he came in. He was looking more pleased with himself than for the last week, but declined to explain what the cause of his good humour was.

"Where have you been all morning, Paul?"

"Oh, just around and about," he said lightly and that was all she could get out of him.

"Pasterwake telephoned," she told him. "He said he expected you at the Dorchester this evening for dinner. Seven thirty and don't change. Someone called Coffee is going to be there too."

"That'll be his chief script writer. His real name's Tchaikowsky."

"I suppose I'm staying at home as usual."

"Yes, darling. I'm afraid you are. This is strictly business."

Temple retired to his study immediately after lunch, leaving stringent instructions that he was not to be disturbed. The telephone exchange was told that no incoming calls would be accepted until six o'clock. Charlie crept about his duties on tip-toe. Steve, not daring to turn on the radio in the sitting toom, listened to Woman's Hour lying flat on her bed with a portable receiver close to her ear. At about four o'clock she rattled the tea things tentatively in case her husband was feeling like a cup of tea but there was no response from the study.

He emerged at ten to six with half a dozen envelopes in his hand and rang for Charlie.

"Is that all you've been doing, Paul; writing letters?"

Temple smiled and shook his head.

"These are only invitation cards."

"Invitations? What to?"

"You and I are going to give a cocktail party, Steve."

"Well, it's nice of you to let me know! When is this to be, or am I expected to conjure olives and anchovies out of mid-air?"

"Don't worry. This cocktail party is going to take care of itself. You're invited, of course, but you won't have to make any preparations." He turned away as Charlie knocked on the door. "Charlie, I want you to go round to the Post Office with these. Try and catch the six o'clock collection, if you can."

"Paul." Steve went up to her husband and took the lapels of his jacket between her fingers. "This means you're pretty near the end, doesn't it?"

"Yes. Pretty near it, I think."

"I'm not going to ask any questions because I know you'll tell me when you think it's right to do so; but you will be careful, won't you?"

"I will. And I'm not trying to be secretive. It's just that I feel you're safer if you don't know too much."

Temple broke away from his dinner engagement as early as he reasonably could but it was already nearly ten when he left the Dorchester.

"Taxi, Mr. Temple?" the Commissionnaire at the door called to him as he came out.

"No thanks, Tom. I have my car."

He got across Park Lane without difficulty. It was a fairly slack time for traffic, between rush hour and the sudden thickening up which coincides with the end of the theatres and cinema programmes. He always preferred to leave his car in the Park rather than become involved in the maze of streets round the Dorchester. The Frazer Nash was not the kind of vehicle that interested thieves. It was too unusual and striking. He had left the hood up and parked her under a lamp standard with the result that the interior was in heavy shadow. He had opened the door and slid behind the wheel before he realised that someone was occupying the passenger's seat.

"All right, Temple," a man's voice said. "Get in and shut that door."

Temple brought his other leg in and closed the door. He did not feel seriously alarmed. He could not bring himself to believe that anyone would attempt murder on this crowded thoroughfare.

"I suggest you start up and drive round past Hyde Park Corner. Keep inside the Park."

Temple inserted his ignition key in the slot and switched on. The engine fired at the first touch on the starter. He selected second gear, glanced over his shoulder and pulled out into the roadway. He went straight through into top gear and let the car idle along at twenty-five miles an hour.

"Forgive my rather informal method of introducing myself," the man said. "It seemed the best way of doing so without attracting undue attention."

"You're Davis, aren't you?"

"Correct. And I assure you I am quite unarmed."

For some reason most of the cars using the Park that evening had some very urgent business awaiting them. They tooted and fussed and flashed their lights in their efforts to pass the Fraser Nash.

"Why don't you go at the same speed as everyone else?" Davis asked nervously. Temple accelerated.

"Does that make you happier?" He glanced at his passenger's hands but they were folded innocently on his stomach. "To what do I owe the pleasure of this surprise? Perhaps you want to collect the taxi fare I owe you?"

"Taxi fare?"

"Yes. The fare for my wife to return home last night."

"Oh, that! Forget it. Mrs. Temple was a charming hostage. But I think she was a little foolhardy, don't you? She might not always get away with it so lightly."

Temple said nothing.

"How have your books been selling lately?" Davis inquired suddenly.

"Not too badly, thank you."

"I think you should confine yourself to literary activities, Mr. Temple. Very few people can make a success of two careers and I am afraid that your taste for amateur detection may land you in serious difficulties."

"You really think so?"

"I'm sure of it. The Tyler mystery is a case in point. I am very much afraid that if you and Mrs. Temple persist in interfering this may be the last case you will ever investigate. Forgive me for saying so, but in my opinion you are completely out of your depth."

"Everyone is entitled to an opinion," Temple said peaceably. "May I ask you your opinion on another matter? Did the murderer of Betty Tyler achieve what he or she wanted by it?"

"I'm not going to answer questions," Davis answered sharply, his voice rising a little. "I'm simply trying to give you a friendly warning. You may think that this is just some girl who's been murdered in a moment of passion. I'm telling you it's something a great deal bigger than that. Something far bigger than you can handle. Take my tip; get out of this and leave the police to do their own work. You'll regret it if you don't."

Hyde Park Corner swam by on their left. Temple pulled

over to leave passing room to a car he could see coming up fast in his mirror.

"You're rather underestimating my intelligence, Mr. Davis, if you think I believe that Betty Tyler, Jane Dallas and Stephen Brooks were all killed in the same moment of passion."

"Stephen Brooks? Then that's why—"

Davis broke off sharply and twisted round in his seat. The approaching car was right on their tail, its headlights blazing into them. There came a crash of gears as the driver clumsily selected third gear and accelerated to pass them. Temple was forced to brake slightly and pull to his left. He saw that the bonnet of the other car was dangerously close and glanced towards the front seat. He had a quick glimpse of a face and a hand clutching a revolver, saw a spurt of flame and felt the bullet crash through the window beside his ear. He braked sharply so that the other car was precipitated ahead. Almost instantly two more shots came crashing through the windscreen, shattering the glass and blurring his view. The Frazer Nash slewed sideways, mounted the pavement and came to rest with a metallic crunch against a lamp standard. From the roadway came the screech of tyres as the cars following behind braked to avoid it.

The glass in the window beside Temple had fallen out. Through the empty frame he saw the attacking car crash the lights at Albert Gate and disappear into Knightsbridge.

For a moment Temple was unable to believe that he was not hurt. He heard a groan beside him and looked round. Davis's head was thrown back; his eyes were shut and he was biting on his lip. His right hand was pressed to his left shoulder as if in an attempt to prevent the blood from spurting out. People were already running towards them. One driver had the presence of mind to bring a fire extinguisher and was aiming it at the Frazer Nash as if daring it to burst into flames. Temple tried to open the door on his side but it was jammed and refused to budge.

"You all right?"

Someone had reached his side of the car and was peering in anxiously.

"I'm O.K. This chap beside me's hurt, though. Can you give a hand and get him out?"

Temple was forced to sit and do nothing while the unofficial rescue party went to work. As usual three Men of Action had emerged, backed up by a greater number of sightseers and advisers.

"Now, stand back, please. Don't crowd in."

"Let's get him out on the pavement where we can have a look at him."

"Did you hear the shots? Must have been car bandits."

"Handle him gently, now. There may be bones broken."

"Is the other one dead?"

"My! Look at all that glass."

"Is there a doctor here?"

"Now, *please* stand back. Can't you see this chap's badly hurt?"

In spite of it all, Davis was extracted from the passenger's seat. He was only wounded in one place and was able to stand up without difficulty. Temple scrambled out after him. Davis was white but he managed to summon up a wry smile.

"Perhaps you're convinced now, Temple. This is the sort of thing I was warning you against."

"That's a nasty wound you've got. Better let me have a look at it right away."

The roar of a motor cycle and the whimper of its tyres as the rider braked brought a sudden silence to the little crowd. Everyone watched while the police patrolman pulled his bike on to the stand and came towards the damaged car, loosening his helmet strap and pulling off his gloves.

"Now then, is the owner of this car here?"

Temple was tempted to give a false name. He did not want Forbes and Vosper to get wind of this incident just yet and he knew that the report of the shooting affray would reach them within the hour. He decided, however, that it would not pay him in the long run to play fast and loose with the Metropolitan Police.

"I'm the owner, Officer," Temple said. He was trying to ease Davis' coat off without causing too much pain. The sleeve was soaked in blood and it was obvious that he was loosing strength fast. "I'll give you my name and address in a moment. Just at the minute I'm more worried about this wound."

"That looks like a bullet wound," the Constable said sharply as Temple ripped Davis' shirt away and exposed the shoulder.

"It is. And on a nasty spot too. It's going to be difficult to put a tourniquet on."

"Here's the ambulance, anyway. They'll take care of him, sir. Now if you'll just give me your account of what happened here— "

The ambulance, its bell shrilling, nosed up through the crowd. The attendants jumped down and ran to Davis. While they laid him down on a stretcher and set about stopping the flow of blood, Temple took the Constable a little on one side.

"My name's Temple," he said. "Paul Temple, 127a, Eaton Square."

The Constable looked at him quickly and then scribbled the name down.

"To put it briefly, we were fired at by a car which passed us and then disappeared into Knightsbridge. A black Ford Zephyr, but I'm afraid I didn't get the number."

"Black Zephyr," the Constable repeated, writing in his notebook.

"Now, this all ties in with a case I'm working on with Inspector Vosper and Sir Graham Forbes. I suggest you tell your Superintendent that when you put your report in. I shall be giving them full details later on. In the meantime I want to stay close to this chap who's been hit. I suppose they'll take him to the Middlesex Hospital."

"Yes, sir. It'll be the Middlesex."

The Constable wrote a few more words in his notebook and glanced doubtfully at Temple.

"I suppose it'll be all right to leave it like that, sir?"

"I promise you it will, Officer." Temple glanced at the number on his tunic. "What's your name? I don't think I've seen you before."

"Grant, sir. I've just been moved from Y Division."

"I'll straighten it out with Sir Graham for you, Grant. Can I leave you to deal with this car? I'm afraid she'll need a breakdown wagon."

The ambulance men were already loading a recumbent Davis into the ambulance. Temple jumped in after him just before the doors were clanged. Less than five minutes had elapsed since the shots had been fired.

Davis' eyes were open. The ambulance attendant grinned at Temple encouragingly.

"You've no call to worry about your friend, sir. The bullet just grazed his shoulder. He's had a bit of a shock and I think he'd better see a doctor, but I don't suppose they'll want to keep him."

As Davis was wheeled down the corridor of the hospital to the surgery Temple spotted a call box near the entrance.

He went inside and dialled his own Eaton Square number. To his relief Steve answered at once.

"Hullo, Steve."

"Paul!" There was only a very brief silence before she said: "Is everything all right?"

"Yes, quite all right. Everything under control your end?"

"Yes, of course. Why?"

"Steve, you won't go out, will you?"

"No. Why on earth should I?"

"Don't answer the door till I get back. And Steve, tell Charlie to shoot the bolts."

"Paul, what on earth has happened?"

"Nothing much. I'll be home quite soon and I'll tell you all about it."

"Be care—" Steve started to say, but he had already rung off.

The doctor who dressed Davis' wound brought him down to where Temple was waiting.

"You're Mr. Temple, are you?"

"Yes."

"I've just been telephoning the police. We have to report cases like this to them, you know. They told me I could let Mr. Davis go as long as he was in your care."

"I'll look after him. The wound wasn't serious?"

"I think he'll be all right," the doctor said. "I'm glad there's someone to see him home, though. He may feel the after-effects of shock. He'd better see his own doctor as soon as he can."

"Thank you very much, doctor," Davis said. "Do I owe you anything?"

"No," the doctor smiled. "This is on the house."

Davis was shaking his head as he walked out into the street with Temple.

"Now I suppose I'll have to start paying my income tax," he said. "Or my conscience will be giving me trouble."

Temple hailed a passing cab and opened the door for Davis.

"Where do you want to go?"

Davis halted with one foot on the step and stared back at Temple.

"Aren't you going to turn me in?"

Temple shook his head.

"Why should I? You told me your warning was a friendly one."

He handed Davis the overcoat which he had been holding on to since the accident.

"In return I'd like to ask you a favour. I'm giving a cocktail party at a hotel in Sonning called "The Dutch Treat" at twelve o'clock on Sunday. I hope you will come. You will find several friends there."

Davis glanced at Temple, as if wondering whether to take him seriously.

"And there's one small question I'd like to ask you. It's really a very simple one."

Davis' face had taken on a more defensive expression. He clearly expected Temple to renew his questions about Betty Tyler.

"Well?"

"When did you buy your overcoat, Mr. Davis?"

CHAPTER TEN

Temple noticed with amusement that Davis had waited till he was out of earshot before giving the taxi driver his instructions. He began to walk towards Oxford Street, hoping that it would not be long before another empty taxi came along. He had gone about a hundred yards when a black ministerial Humber turned into his street and accelerated rapidly towards the entrance of the Middlesex Hospital. Temple glanced at the number plate, then stepped out into the road and waved a hand. The Humber was almost past him when the driver braked hard and drew up at the kerbside. Temple walked across towards the car. The rear seat passenger was already lowering his window.

"Hullo, Temple," Sir Graham said. "I only got the report ten minutes ago. I collected Vosper and came round as quickly as I could. You're not hurt, are you?"

Sir Graham's driver had nipped out to open the door. In answer to the unspoken invitation, Temple stooped to climb in. Vosper transferred himself to one of the foldaway chairs in the back of the partition so as to leave room for Temple beside Sir Graham.

"We heard that the man who was with you was hit, sir," he said. "Who was it?"

"Davis. He was waiting in my car when I came out from the Dorchester at about a quarter to ten. He said he wanted to give me a friendly warning to keep my nose out of the Tyler mystery."

"Impudent blighter!" observed Sir Graham.

"We'd got a little further than Hyde Park Corner when a car came past rather too close for comfort. The front seat passenger fired three revolver shots and I'm afraid I put the Frazer Nash into a lamp post. They missed me but they got Davis."

"So they've started gunning for you, have they?"

"It's very obliging of Davis to play into our hands like this," Vosper remarked. "Will the hospital authorities agree to release him? If so we can put him in right away."

"I'm sorry to say you can't."

"Oh? He's really bad, is he?"

"No. It was only a flesh wound, as they say. I sent him home in a taxi."

"You what?"

After a moment of outraged silence, Sir Graham said: "Keep calm, Inspector. I'm confident Temple can tell us where to find him."

"I'm afraid not," Temple answered equably. "I didn't hear what address he gave the taxi driver."

"You mean to tell us, sir, that you had this man, who kidnapped your wife and tried to decoy you into a murder trap, in the palm of your hand and you let him go like that—"

"Just a minute, Inspector," Sir Graham cut in. "Temple, I think you owe us a full explanation of this extraordinary behaviour of yours. As I think I remarked last night, this is a very difficult and serious case—"

"Sir Graham, it is because this is such a serious and difficult case that I am behaving in what you call an extraordinary way. But I agree that you are entitled to some explanation. Since there's nothing for us at the Middlesex Hospital, could you possibly run me back to the flat? I haven't a car and I want to get back to Steve as soon as I can."

Sir Graham unhooked the speaking tube that connected him with his driver and pulled out the stopper.

"Drive to Eaton Square, Stokes, please."

Temple leaned back as the car glided forward. He pulled out his case and after Sir Graham and Vosper had refused one helped himself to a cigarette.

"You know that saying: 'When thieves fall out wise men tremble'?"

Vosper grunted. Sir Graham did not answer.

"I believe that is the key to the murder of Stephen Brooks."

"You mean that he was the victim of some sort of gang warfare? What about Betty Tyler and Jane Dallas? They don't seem very likely members of a gang to me."

"This is rather an unusual gang, Sir Graham." The graveness with which he spoke was not lost on his two listeners. "Personally I would rather not use that word at all. I would prefer to call it conspiracy. But those two girls were not involved in criminal activities. As a result of their personal associations and through no fault of their own they came into possession of facts so vitally important to the conspiracy that their silence had to be assured by the only permanent method. As for Stephen Brooks, I believe he was murdered because of his associations with me. I have a feeling that he was tempted to reveal the whole thing to me and might have done so if he had been allowed to live."

Sir Graham ruminated for a moment.

"You say that your proverb is the key to the murder of Brooks. Why not also to the murder of Betty Tyler? It was the first crime in the series."

"It's my belief that her death was not the result of what you call gang warfare, but the cause of it."

"I don't quite follow you, sir," Vosper said, holding on to the door handle as the car swung round a corner.

"I mean that her murder split the conspirators into two groups. It is the only explanation that accounts for the violent developments we have witnessed."

The Park was still open and their driver had chosen to take the Ring road. Temple leaned forward as they passed the spot where his car had crashed. He saw that Constable Grant had done his stuff and that the wrecked Frazer Nash had been taken away. All that was left to show the scene of the shooting was one very bent lamp standard.

"Temple," Sir Graham said. "You know who killed these people, don't you? Why not come into the open and tell us?"

Temple drew deep on his cigarette before answering.

"Yes. I know who strangled Betty Tyler and Jane Dallas and coshed Stephen Brooks. What's more he damned nearly had me this evening too. I saw his face at the window of that Ford Zephyr just before the first shot was fired."

Vosper leaned forward and a crimson glare silhouetted the deep lines of his face for a moment. The car had halted before the red traffic light on Knightsbridge.

"I don't know this man's real name. The only time I met him formally he introduced himself as Garry Brooks. I've seen him on two other occasions; once at Sonning shortly after he'd tried to force me under a brick lorry, and once this evening."

"You can give me a description of him, then, sir?"

"Yes, Inspector, I can. I'll make you out a full description according to the usual police formula. I'd like to be able to provide you with fingerprints too, but the *soi-disant* Mr. Brooks took great care not to touch anything while he was in my flat. In fact that was what first made me suspicious of him."

"I wonder why you didn't tell us all this before, Temple." Sir Graham spoke a little stiffly. "If we can obtain our evidence against this man our case will be concluded. As it is we have enough to arrest him on. He may break down under examination."

"I'm afraid it's not as simple as that, Sir Graham. This man – let's call him Garry for want of a better name – is only a hired thug. The person behind these murders, the person who planned and ordered them and upon whom the real guilt rests is going to be very much harder to nail."

"You know who it is?"

"I have a very shrewd idea," Temple said. "But not a grain of evidence to support it."

After another short silence Sir Graham spoke again, but his tone was less reserved.

"In view of what you say we must put out a general call for this Garry person without delay. The moment Vosper has your description—"

"I agree with you there. Several lives are in danger as long as he remains at large. But I would strongly suggest leaving Davis alone, though you could check with the police at Cape Town. They might possibly throw some light on his activities when he was there about a year ago."

"You must have had quite a cosy chat, you two," Vosper remarked drily. "Did he tell you his life story?"

Temple smiled. "Not exactly, but I noticed that his overcoat bore the label of a Cape Town outfitter and he informed me that he'd had it about a year."

The car had turned into Eaton Square. Sir Graham's driver had assumed that their destination was the Temples' flat. He cruised slowly along the quiet roadway and stopped opposite number 127a.

"You'll come in for a drink, won't you?"

Sir Graham shook his head.

"I must get back to my office, I'm afraid. The Tyler murder isn't the only unsolved crime in the country, is it, Inspector?"

Vosper snorted. He put his fingers on the handle of the door but did not open it.

"Before you go, sir. You will telephone me that description at once, won't you?"

"I promise you it's the first thing I'll do, Inspector."

"And just one more point. You told Sir Graham that you had a good idea who the instigator of these murders is, but nothing to prove it. Do you anticipate finding any proof?"

"I said I expected to indicate this person to you on Sunday. That promise still holds good."

Vosper nodded and opened the door. Temple was standing on the pavement about to say goodbye, when Sir Graham leant forward.

"There is one important factor which you haven't mentioned, Temple. That slip of paper we found on Brooks with the words 'Crown Jewel'. Just where does that come in?"

"Where that comes in," Temple said with a smile, "is something we shall all know by tomorrow night."

He closed the car door gently and turned towards the flat.

Steve was startled when her husband put his head round the bedroom door next morning. He was wearing the trousers of a suit which he only wore for sporting occasions.

"Put on something gay," he advised her. "You and I are going down to Windsor."

"To Windsor? Are you presenting me at court?"

"No. The Berkshire Stakes are being run on the race course there this afternoon. I have a couple of good grandstand tickets."

Steve turned to look at him doubtfully.

"Paul, don't you feel we'd be letting Sir Graham down rather? He's absolutely counting on you in this Tyler case."

Temple gave the matter a moment's thought.

"I feel we need to get away from the Tyler mystery for a bit, Steve; stand back and view it from afar, so to speak. After all, we've thought of nothing else for the last ten days and I for one am beginning to feel a bit stale."

He went back into his dressing room to fetch a gay bow tie and stood in the doorway while he knotted it.

"Besides, you've been pestering me for a new fur cape all year."

"I suppose we're going to shoot a mink in the Great Park on the way home?"

"No. But I have a hot tip for you. You can stake ten

pounds and if it comes in first you'll have that mink stole."

Halfway through breakfast the telephone rang and a minute later Charlie was at the dining room door.

"Sir Graham to speak to you, Mr. Temple."

Temple chewed hard on his mouthful of toast and marmalade and managed to swallow most of it before he took up the receiver. Sir Graham, for once in his life, sounded almost excited.

"Temple? I have some news for you. You remember you asked me if it would be possible to raid Tomlinson's place?"

"Yes."

"Well, for rather an odd reason we have been able to do so. His premises were broken into last night. He must have surprised the intruders; he was beaten up rather badly, and only just managed to drag himself to the telephone. A less tough nut would have been dead."

"Any idea what time this happened?"

"Between three and four a.m."

Conscious of the sudden silence on the line Sir Graham said: "Are you still there?"

"Yes. I was just working it out. He could just have done it."

"Who could?"

"Our friend Garry. He must have had a pretty busy evening yesterday. I suppose no one saw a black Ford Zephyr in the area?"

"We'll check that point. I was rather doubtful whether our friend could have got down there in time."

"A ruthless driver could easily maintain an average of fifty during the night. I suppose you'll put checks on all the roads leading back towards London."

"We have," Sir Graham said wearily. "But I'm not too confident in their efficacy. You remember how easily Shelford eluded us. Incidentally, Vosper is on his way round to see you. He thinks he's identified the man who shot at you last night. He has a record as long as your arm."

"Good. That's something positive at last. I gather the police took the chance to search Tomlinson's place. Did they find anything interesting?"

"I don't know whether you'll think it's interesting or not, Temple. You'll appreciate that we haven't had time to send anyone down there yet. We're working on the report from the County Police. They say they found something that looks damned like an illicit still for brewing hooch."

"I think that's very interesting indeed, Sir Graham. Any more sign of those leaves they found in the Thames Warehouse – the ones that suggested tobacco to Vosper?"

"Curiously enough, yes." Sir Graham's voice sounded puzzled. "The C.I.D. man who made the search said that there had been a stack of these leaves. He came to the conclusion that the object of the raid was to pinch them. He found bits scattered on the ground leading out to where the car was parked."

Steve opened the door quietly and peeped in. Guessing that the conversation was going to be a long one she had brought his coffee so that he could drink it before it became cold. She put it down beside the telephone and he smiled his thanks.

"It would be worth asking a botanist to examine those leaves, Sir Graham. What does Tomlinson say about it all?"

"He denies knowledge of any tobacco leaves and explains the brewery by saying he was interested in chemical experiments. Rather thin, of course, but severe concussion is not the best aid to telling convincing lies. . . . Just a moment, Temple—"

Sir Graham broke off. Temple heard him talking faintly on another telephone. He had time to finish his cup before Sir Graham picked up the receiver.

"Temple, I have to go over to the Home Office in a hurry. I'll contact you later. By the way, what's all this nonsense about a cocktail party down at Sonning tomorrow? Vosper had an invitation too. You know we haven't got time to go gadding down to the country with a thing like this on our hands. Even the Minister is starting to flap now."

"I'm sorry you can't come, Sir Graham," Temple said politely. "Because I was going to introduce you to the person behind all these murders."

*

Vosper arrived very shortly afterwards. He glanced critically at Temple's country suit and bright bow tie, then produced a small photograph from his pocket.

"Is that him?"

Temple stared hard at the features which had been mercilessly recorded full face and profile, under the flash-bulb of the police photographer.

"That's Master Garry, all right."

"Good." Vosper heaved an immense sigh of relief. "We had quite a job digging him out. He's a real bad hat, this one; car-jack, cosher, slasher, shakester, the lot. He's been inside twice already. Now we have your identification we'll put out a general call for him. His real name is Nash. William Nash."

Temple cast back in his mind, searching for a memory.

"The Wolfson Extortion Case?"

"That's him. I always believed it was Nash who killed Constable Pettiward, but they couldn't pin it on him. Well, sir—" Vosper took the photograph back and returned it to his wallet. "As Lady Godiva said: 'Thank heaven we're nearing our close'."

"You're coming to my party at 'The Dutch Treat' tomorrow, Inspector?"

Vosper shook his head disapprovingly and pursed his lips.

"Can't spare the time, sir. We're far too busy. Thank you for the invitation, all the same."

"I should consult Sir Graham, Inspector. I think you'll find he's changed his mind."

That same morning Mick Tyler had welcomed the coming of daylight with relief. It delivered her from the unavailing struggle to sleep and the dreadful images that flooded her mind whenever she closed her eyes. She had dressed and breakfasted long before she heard the tramp of the postman on her deck and saw the single white envelope which fluttered down the flight of steps. She stooped to pick it up, stared at the handwriting and ripped it open. It contained a plain white card.

> Mr. and Mrs. Paul Temple
> request the pleasure
> of your company at
> "The Dutch Treat", Sonning.
> Cocktails 12-1 p.m.

A postscript had been added underneath.

"I hope you will come, Mrs. Tyler. This is what you have been waiting for. A car will call for you at eleven."

After making the customary round of his Mayfair Salon, Mariano turned into his own luxuriously furnished office. He pressed the buzzer on his desk and after a moment his secretary entered. She was a trim blonde girl of about twenty-five with an exquisite figure and the carriage of a duchess. She brought a notebook, a pencil and Mariano's morning mail.

"I don't know that I should have opened this, Mr. Mariano. It wasn't marked Personal."

She placed a square card in front of her employer. Mariano read Temple's invitation quickly, and smiled at his secretary.

"That's quite all right, Miss Longman. Mr. Paul Temple is a personal friend of mine, you know."

George Westeral had returned to London for the weekend and was staying in the suite which he habitually occupied in the Berkeley Hotel. He had been out on a party till 3 a.m. and slept solidly till ten o'clock when a waiter knocked on his door. Westeral grunted and the man brought in a breakfast tray with four newspapers and his mail.

The waiter, who knew the form, put the tray down on the table beside his bed, drew the curtains and turned on the taps so that the water began to dribble into the bath. Long experience had shown that this adjustment would provide a bath of the correct temperature in about thirty minutes. Westeral poured himself a cup of coffee and glanced at the headlines of the paper before turning to the half-dozen envelopes propped beside the toast rack. Four of them were bills. The fifth was Temple's invitation.

Underneath the formal words had been added this short message:

"I am asking all those interested in Betty Tyler's murder and thought that you would like to be present."

Tomlinson's housekeeper was in a fine rage. In the course of their investigations the police had brought a great deal of mud and muck into the usually spotless house. Her resentment against all forms of uniformed authority broke over the innocent Davidstown postman like a tidal wave.

"Anyone would think he was a criminal," she stormed. "It's adding insult to injury, that's what it is. What's all this rubbish you've brought?"

She took a fistful of envelopes from the postman and glanced through them quickly.

"He'll not want to be bothered with such things at a time like this."

So Temple's carefully worded invitation, together with a Final Demand from the Commissioners of Inland Revenue and sundry Statements of Account, went into the waste-paper basket.

Temple conveyed Steve down to Windsor in a Drive Yourself Hire Car. She had taken literally the invitation to wear something gay and had even made a quick expedition up to Knightsbridge to buy herself a new hat.

It was a perfect day for racing. A faint breeze was

blowing across the Thames and the turf, enclosed by the white-painted rails, was a vivid, succulent green. The stands and enclosures were filled to capacity; above the exciting crowd-murmur which precedes a race rose the cries of the bookmakers shouting the odds. Steve and Temple arrived in time to see the runners go out to the start of the first race, the brilliant shirts of the jockeys bobbing on horses that danced as lightly as ballerinas.

Steve picked out her favourite colours in the next two races and lost ten shillings on the Tote. The fourth race was the Berkshire Stakes. Scarcely was the previous event over before Temple led Steve towards the enclosure where most of the bookies were congregated.

"I want you to get your bet on early," he told her.

The bookies were just chalking the names of the horses up on their boards. Temple selected a bookmaker whom he'd seen at race meetings before and stood with Steve watching him complete his list. He handed his wife two five pound notes.

"Put that on 'Crown Jewel'."

Steve started forward, then turned back to search Paul's face.

"Crown Jewel? Those were the words written on the paper they found in Stephen Brooks' pocket."

"I realise that."

"Was it just a racing tip, then?"

"We shall soon know. You go and lay your bet."

The odds against Crown Jewel were forty to one. He watched Steve walk shyly up to the enormous bookie, offer her money and receive a ticket in return.

"Shall we go back to the stand now, Paul? We can see better from there."

"No. I want to stay here for a bit."

The business of betting was going on steadily all round them. Now and then the bookies would rub out a figure and replace it with another while a steady stream of punters sidled up and laid their bets. A mysterious unifying influence seemed to keep control over the whole business as the bookies glanced round to study the gestures of the tic-tac man.

About ten minutes before the start a curious invisible wind seemed to move across the assembly. The bookies, like a herd of bison that scents an enemy on the air, started turning their heads uneasily. The odds against Crown Jewel had shortened to thirty to one. Now they fell at a bump to fifteen to one. A minute later, while the spit was still wet on the boards, the fifteen had been rubbed out and replaced by a seven.

Steve stared at Paul in astonishment.

"Was all that because I put ten pounds on him?"

"No. It means that at the last minute Crown Jewel was heavily backed to win a very large sum of money. Come on, let's get back to our seats."

Crown Jewel finally started at five to one. He didn't

show amongst the leaders till the last three furlongs. Then, with an electrifying burst of speed, he came tearing up on the outside and won by two lengths.

"By Timothy, Steve!" Temple shouted above the din. "We've done it! We've done it!"

Beside him Steve was jumping up and down in excitement.

"I've won four hundred pounds! Paul, you must take me racing more often."

CHAPTER ELEVEN

Steve was unusually silent as the little party drove to Sonning in the same hired car next morning. She and Temple occupied the front seats and Charlie, with a white waiter's coat and an automatic pistol in the suitcase beside him, rode in the back. The spell of brilliant weather had ended and this Sunday morning was dull and muggy under a layer of heavy grey cloud.

It was about twenty to twelve when they entered the built up area of Sonning. A string of twenty cars or so was lined up outside the parish church and from inside came faint hymnal sounds.

"I wish I didn't have this odd feeling that something awful is going to happen," Steve remarked suddenly. "Do you have to go through with it, Paul?"

"It's too late to change our minds now. This is a risk I've got to take." Temple glanced over his shoulder. "You've checked that automatic, Charlie?"

"Yes, sir," Charlie replied in his most business-like voice. "You've no call to worry, Mrs. Temple. I'll keep my eyes skinned."

"If only I knew which of them is the murderer, Paul. It's this uncertainty that's so wearing."

"I'm not telling anyone that," Temple said firmly. "Not even Sir Graham. You might betray yourselves by some look or even thought and then I'd lose the element of surprise on which I'm relying – And Steve—"

"Yes."

"You may think my performance at this cocktail party is a piece of inexcusable exhibitionism, but I promise you it's necessary if I'm to achieve my purpose."

He turned away from the road for a moment to grin at Steve encouragingly.

"Cheer up, darling. It'll soon be over."

"I know," she said glumly. "That's just it."

Lucille Draper was waiting for them at the entrance to "The Dutch Treat". She was dressed very soberly in black and wore no ornaments or jewellery. She answered Temple's greeting with a wan smile and came slowly forward to meet him.

"Is everything arranged?" he asked.

"Everything is fixed exactly as you explained, Mr. Temple. The room is on the top floor. Your guests will be directed up there by my staff. Was I right in thinking that you were bringing your own waiter?"

"Yes. Charlie here will do the job. Shall we go up right away? They should be arriving soon."

Since it was not yet opening time the car park and the hotel itself were still fairly empty. Mrs. Draper led them along a corridor to the lift which was one of the improvements she had made during her ownership. The doors moved smoothly to and fro and they glided up to the fourth floor.

"I've given you the sitting room of one of my suites," Lucille Draper explained, opening the door of a large room with a broad French window. A table covered with a white cloth and laden with bottles and glasses had been placed across one corner. "You want me to stay, don't you?"

"Yes, please," Temple said. "But as my guest, of course. Charlie, you'd better get to work."

Charlie crouched down behind the drinks table to open his suitcase. Temple tested the door leading through from the bedroom and found it locked. He opened the windows and stepped out on to the balcony which extended far enough to include the bedroom belonging to the same suite.

"What an attractive room!" Steve said to Mrs. Draper. "I hope we can come and stay here one day."

"I hope so too," she replied, her eyes moving to Temple's face.

It was still a minute before twelve when the first knock on the door came. One of the hotel waiters opened it and showed in Mick Tyler. For once she was dressed in a skirt, but it did little to mitigate her habitual masculinity. She was paler than usual. After nodding briefly to Temple and his wife her eyes swung to Lucille Draper.

"This is Mrs. Draper," Temple said by the way of introduction. "Mrs. Tyler."

"Haven't I heard that name before?"

"You have," Steve confirmed with a smile. "But this is the real one."

Charlie came forward with his tray of drinks and had to swerve as the door opened again. Davis came in full of confidence and dressed in a black double-breasted suit with a very strong pin stripe. One arm was parcelled away under his coat and the empty sleeve had been tucked neatly into a pocket. He gave off a faint aroma of some subtle perfume. He and Mick Tyler eyed each other rather shyly as if in doubt whether they knew each other or not. It was with great relief that Davis turned to Charlie and helped himself to a cocktail.

Sir Graham and Vosper arrived in company with Mariano who had the look of a well-bred poodle who finds himself flanked by a couple of shaggy sheep dogs. His light grey suit was impeccable and the customary carnation was in his buttonhole. Sir Graham had managed to combine tweediness with elegance and Vosper in his Sunday clothes looked very unpolicemanlike.

Sir Graham's resonant voice and man-of-the-worldliness provided a kind of cover or backcloth; soon the rather uneasy-little groups had broken up and the gathering began to resemble a real cocktail party.

Last of all to arrive was Westeral. He wore a hacking

jacket and a pair of cavalry twill trousers with narrow legs. He looked round the faces turned towards him, rather surprised to find himself invited to this odd gathering but too well-mannered to show it.

"Mr. Westeral, you know my wife, Sir Graham and the Inspector here. I don't think you've met Mrs. Tyler. And may I introduce Mrs. Draper, Mr. Davis and Mr. Mariano?"

Westeral nodded to each in turn, his hands pressed to the outside of his jacket pockets. He picked out Sir Graham and moved over to engage him in conversation. Temple closed the door and confirmed with a quick glance that there were ten people in the room.

Steve was moving about with the ease of a skilful hostess, making sure that no one was left out, while Charlie kept an eye on their glasses. To the casual observer it might have been a perfectly ordinary Sunday morning drink party, but Steve sensed the atmosphere of tension and knew that everyone there was acting a part and waiting.

Temple accepted a cocktail from Charlie and turned to face Mariano who had weaved his way towards him.

"Mr. Temple, I was delighted to receive your invitation but now that I am here I wonder whether I should have accepted. Am I mistaken or are most of those present associated in some way with the case which you are investigating – the Tyler mystery?"

A sudden hush had fallen on the gathering, so that the last three words fell into a pool of silence. Everyone's head had turned towards Temple and private conversations were abruptly forgotten.

"You are not mistaken, Mr. Mariano, and in fact all those present are connected with the Tyler mystery."

Steve felt her heart begin to pound and thought: "This is it."

Temple moved a little way to put his glass down on a table. The movement brought him in front of his guests who now formed a rough semi-circle round him. Charlie had moved quietly to his post outside the circle, behind the drinks table and close to the door.

"Since everyone has arrived," Temple said, "we may as well come to the matter we are here to discuss. Unfortunately two guests whom I would like to have welcomed are unable to be here. Mr. Tomlinson met with an accident and Mr. William Nash is unavoidably detained at – Bow Street is it, Sir Graham?"

Sir Graham grunted in confirmation. Mick Tyler and Davis moved a little closer together as if seeking mutual support.

"What I am going to say," Temple went on, "will not make very pleasant hearing for any of you. I am going to expose a fraud and make accusations against many of those present. But" – here he paused to let his words sink in – "I am only going to accuse one person of murder. So unless you have murder on your conscience, it will pay you to hear me out."

He glanced towards Vosper and saw him nod slightly in appreciation of this strategic move.

"Very soon after I began to interest myself in the murder of Betty Tyler, and shortly afterwards of her friend Jane Dallas, I became convinced that their deaths were due to the fact that they had touched the fringes of some illegal organisation. To solve the mystery of their deaths, I felt, it would be necessary to discover what form this organisation took."

Watching her husband Steve realised that he was choosing his words with great care, as if he were already making out his case in a court of law. That he held the attention of his listeners there was no doubt. All their eyes were fixed on his face.

"What struck me as odd was that the people who were implicated did not belong to a class or type which one usually associates with organised crime. Yet they all had two things in common: a deep seated need for money and an unexplained source of income."

Temple's eyes roved round the half circle of faces and came to rest on Westeral.

"The Honourable George Westeral, raised in the lap of luxury by a loving mother who spoiled her only child and refused him nothing. She even had to engage a private tutor because he couldn't face the idea of boarding school. When his family lost all their money he found himself heir to a title and penniless. Loving luxury and society life, surrounded by rich friends, he sought desperately for some means, any means, of laying his hands on money."

Westeral had gone very pale. He started to say something and then, seeing Temple's glance move away from him, decided to remain silent.

"Mrs. Draper, whose husband, contrary to popular belief, died leaving her an insurance policy barely adequate to cover his debts. She bought "The Dutch Treat" on borrowed capital. For her the credit squeeze was an almost mortal blow. She suddenly found that she had to have more money than the hotel was at that time making. She turned to the only quarter from which she could expect help."

Lucille Draper did not look towards Temple. She stared out of the window with a peaceful, almost proud expression. Steve found it hard to see in her the woman they had met on their first visit to "The Dutch Treat".

"Stephen Brooks was an art connoisseur and a lover of beautiful things. They always cost money."

Temple restrained a faint smile as he turned towards Davis. "I hope Mr. Davis will forgive me if I say simply that he has always loved money and has never been too particular about where it comes from."

Davis shrugged his uninjured shoulder and made a noncommittal expression.

"Mrs. Tyler needed less money but she needed it more urgently. Left to bring up a daughter on her own she struggled to give her a good education. She was determined that before she died she would buy Betty her own business and this passionate desire blinded her to what she was doing. Though he did not know her she knew George Westeral and it was she who engineered the first meeting between Betty and him. You would have liked your daughter to become a peeress, wouldn't you, Mrs. Tyler? Even if her husband came by his money rather irregularly."

Westeral took a hand out of his pocket and ground his cigarette out on an ash tray.

"Don't you think you ought to be more careful what you say about people, Temple? There is such a thing as a law of slander in this country and I have plenty of witnesses here."

"You can take me to court, Mr. Westeral, and if I can't prove what I say I'll stand my term of imprisonment."

"Then I damned well will," Westeral said angrily.

Temple nodded curtly and from then ignored Westeral.

"In addition to this ill-assorted collection – and perhaps others whom the police will discover later – the organisation included two criminals who had previous records, though they were very different from each other – Harry Shelford and William Nash."

Temple took a sip from his drink and ran a hand over the back of his head. Only to Steve was it apparent that he was under a terrific strain.

"The next question was: what was the purpose of this organisation? A series of quite small points, many of which did not strike me as significant at the time, led me gradually towards the answer. On my first visit here I was merely amused to see that the clerk kept a copy of Ruff's *Guide to the Turf* beside his desk. But after that it was remarkable how often I came across something to do with horse racing. It was at the Auteuil race course that Mariano saw Betty Tyler in Paris. I noticed that Tomlinson owned a racing stable. A car park ticket for the Goodwood meeting was pasted on the windshield of Westeral's car. The long-absent Mr. Tyler had been a bookmaker. That was why the words 'Crown Jewel', written on a piece of paper found in Stephen Brooks pocket, suggested a race-horse to me. Yesterday at Windsor Steve put ten pounds on 'Crown Jewel' and it won four hundred. If she'd bet five hundred she would have won twenty thousand. My accountant tells me that to have that sum left after Income Tax had been deducted each year, a man would have to earn astronomical sums. You can see that any foreknowledge of racing results can mean untold wealth to those in the know."

Vosper had sat down abruptly and begun to write furiously in a notebook. Sir Graham was looking fierce but intrigued.

"You mean to say, Temple, that this is just another case of race-horse doping?"

"Something much more subtle than that, Sir Graham.

Say rather a sensationally efficacious diet: a new food which gives a horse energy and stamina and is undetectable even by experts in doping. What is more, without even the connivance of trainers and stable lads it can be added to the feed of any horse in training, unknown to its owner. Of course, the system was not foolproof, but if even half the horses you back come in amongst the first three, you're a rich man—"

"This is a pretty tall order, you know Temple. A sensational new diet—"

"Don't forget, Sir Graham, that Harry Shelford was a chemist. Now I'll explain later how I know this, but I can assure you that in his travels in South Africa he found that some of the tribes used a herbal mixture, based on the leaves of a tobacco-like plant they call docher, to stimulate their animals and give them energy. He very quickly realised that this discovery, if applied to race-horses, could mean a fortune for him or anyone else he let in on the secret. It was a far more effective device than mere doping, because it was undetectable. Indeed, though the Jockey Club would hardly countenance it, I'm not sure that it's even illegal. But it was essential that the secret should remain in the hands of a very few, hence the smuggling and the secrecy."

A kind of unrest had spread over the group. Those present had in an indefinable way split into two groups; the Temples, Charlie, the police officers on the one hand

and the conspirators, to use Temple's word, on the other. No one however attempted to deny the truth of what had been said.

"Shelford's part in the organisation was to obtain supplies of docher and other herbs and to introduce them into this country. He was, so to speak, the overseas representative and forwarding agent. Unfortunately for everyone," Temple continued gravely, "it was also necessary to enrol in the organisation a former jockey turned criminal. This man was William Nash, whose past record shows that he would not stop short even at murder."

He broke off suddenly. Steve had been watching Mick Tyler and now she moved quickly towards her. The older woman had sunk down on to the arm of a chair, her face covered with her hands. She made no sound but seemed to be fighting something behind that barrier. All at once her hand came forward and gripped Steve's arm. She half stood up, her face twisted.

"What is it, Mrs. Tyler? Are you in pain?"

"Tablets in my bag."

The words were choked out. Vosper snatched up her huge black handbag and rooted about in it till he found a small bottle of tablets. He examined them closely before handing them to Steve.

"I hope this is all right," he muttered. Mrs Tyler had sunk back in the deep arm chair. With the help of a glass of water brought by Charlie she managed to get the tablets down. In a few moments her breathing became easier.

She murmured: "Be all right now. Please go on, Mr. Temple."

The little gathering in the room had regrouped itself. Steve sat on the arm of Mick Tyler's chair with Westeral beside her. Lucille Draper had moved nearer to the window. Mariano, his face puckered with worry, accosted Temple as he went back to his place.

"I still do not understand why I am brought here, Mr. Temple. You say everyone has some connection with the murder and you speak about some gang—"

"Mr. Mariano," Temple interrupted. "You are here as my employer. You asked me to solve the Tyler mystery, do you remember? I think you are entitled to be here when I name the murderer, don't you agree? And that, ladies and gentlemen, is what I propose to do in a very few minutes."

The silence in the room was so intense that the sounds from outside were magnified. The bars downstairs had been open for some time and an occasional shout of laughter drifted up. Cars were continually driving into the car park and each arrival was indicated by a volley of slamming doors. Everyone had again focused their attention on Temple. Only one of those present noticed the shadow that crossed the balcony or saw the sudden stirring of the window curtain as a form moved behind it.

"It was because Betty Tyler came into possession of this knowledge that she was killed. She had to share her secret with someone and since Jane Dallas had become her confidante the second girl was also marked down for murder. One member of the organisation had decided that the risk of committing murder was preferable to certain exposure and the loss of an irreplaceable source of income."

Temple paused and for a moment his eyes rested on the window curtain, now hanging completely motionless. Steve looked round the ring of faces. Whichever one of them it is, she thought, must be simply holding on now, hoping against hope that Paul is going to make a mistake.

"I believe that these killings shocked and horrified the other members of the organisation. They may not have known that William Nash's was the hand that actually committed three inhuman crimes, but they were pretty certain that they knew the identity of the person who had coerced him into doing so, the person who bore the moral responsibility for the murders. The organisation split. The two murderers were isolated. The other members could not denounce them without betraying themselves, but they could make sure that their source of income was stopped. They decided on re-routing their supplies and bringing them in by air to Crows Farm."

Temple glanced towards Mick Tyler and a little of the hardness went out of his expression.

"Perhaps more than one person dreamed of a personal vengeance on the murderer of Betty Tyler."

"Sir Graham!"

Everyone's head swung towards Westeral. Ignoring Temple he had turned to Sir Graham Forbes. His expression was that of a man who had tried to be long-suffering but has reached the limit of his patience.

"Is there any law which compels a peaceful citizen to listen to outrageous charges such as have been made here to-day, without any basis of proof whatsoever? I take it that since you have made no attempt to stop all this you associate yourself with Mr. Temple."

Sir Graham seemed uncomfortable but he answered firmly enough:

"Like yourself I am a guest here, Mr. Westeral. I don't believe there is any compulsion on you to remain if you don't wish to, and whether you wish to take legal action against Temple is a matter for you and your solicitors."

"I hope you won't go now, Westeral," Temple put in quickly. "I am just coming to the part which I think will interest you more than any of the others because it concerns you most closely."

The two men glared challengingly into each other's eyes. Westeral broke the tension by stooping to take a cigarette from the box on the table and lighting it with his free hand. Taking this as a sign that his guest had decided to remain, Temple resumed his argument.

"My problem, then, had narrowed itself down to this: which member of the organisation had murdered Betty Tyler? This question led me to another one: who stood to lose most if the plot were uncovered? Admittedly they would all lose a useful source of income, but most of them had achieved their main objects; and the legal charges which could have been made against them were not so desperately grave. But one man faced not only penury but social ostracism, expulsion from his clubs, the loss of all his friends and disgrace on an old family name. What is more, he had suffered an unbearable affront to his self-assurance for when Betty Tyler found out the source of his income she left him in disgust."

The stem of Westeral's glass snapped as his fist clenched on it. He threw the pieces on the floor behind him and turned on Temple with a face the colour of cement. His cheeks and the flesh round the corner of his mouth were trembling.

"Am I to understand that you are accusing me of her murder?"

"I am."

A curious change had come over the gathering. Now that Temple had named his man the tension lessened. Yet there was something purposeful about the way the others watched and listened. They were in some odd way like a jury, following the arguments of counsel, yet already convinced in their minds of the guilt of the accused.

"You forget that I can prove I was nowhere near Oxford when the crime was committed."

"You are still just as guilty as if you had strangled Betty

Tyler with your own hands. You conceived the crime, condoned it and helped to conceal the identity of the killer. The jury will find you equally guilty with William Nash."

Westeral stood shocked as if his face had been slapped.

"I suppose your friends the police will force Nash to make some statement that seems to incriminate me. I don't think any jury will take the word of a convicted criminal against mine." He made an attempt at a laugh. "Why don't you go ahead and accuse me of organising the attempt to kill you the night before last?"

"That was not an attempt to kill me," Temple pointed out. "Davis was the intended victim. Nash was determined that you and he alone should possess this secret; once launched he was prepared to stop at nothing to achieve his ends. In fact it was only the alertness of the river police that foiled his attempt to board Mrs. Tyler's barge early this morning."

Westeral had recovered his self-control a little.

"Sir Graham, I am astonished that you should have allowed this to go so far. These accusations are ridiculous and unfounded. Does anyone seriously believe that I would have come here to-day if I were guilty?"

He swung back towards Temple, undisguised hatred in his eyes.

"Even a child who had followed this case in the papers could point out the fallacy in your arguments. What about Shelford? Why isn't he here to account for himself? You have not mentioned the telephone calls Betty was receiving before her death nor the fact that both she and Jane Dallas had appointments to meet him. Still, I suppose it was natural for you to pick on someone else when you couldn't lay hands on the real murderer."

Mick Tyler had sat up and was following the argument with earnest intentness, her eyes swinging from one speaker to the other. Vosper had begun to edge his way inch by inch nearer to the door.

"Even before the murder," Temple answered calmly, "you were trying to draw suspicion on to Shelford. Since his part in the organisation kept him absent on the Continent and unable to defend himself he was the most suitable suspect. It was you who made those entries in the girls' note books which led the police off on the wrong track. And then you conceived your brilliant idea of a double bluff – a refinement of the technique of planting suspicion. You thought that if it seemed as if someone else was trying to plant suspicion on you, you would appear all the more innocent. So you had your own number put on Nash's car when he forced us off the road ten days ago, knowing that a police check up would show that you owned a Bentley and not a Triumph. I am sorry to have to tell you, Westeral, that this stunning device was the first thing that made me suspect you."

Westeral stubbed out his cigarette and glanced round the room. He saw that all the faces turned towards him were uncompromisingly hostile. For a full thirty seconds he remained in that stooped position. Then he straightened up and turned back to Temple. His voice when he spoke was almost confident.

"You haven't an atom of evidence to justify all this."

Temple said: "Haven't I?"

He looked at Westeral for a long, defiant moment, then he turned to Lucille Draper.

"Mrs. Draper, I think the time has come."

Lucille Draper nodded. She looked towards the open window.

"Harry, you can come in now."

The curtain moved and from behind it there stepped a small man whose age was difficult to guess. His features were sharp and mischievous, his skin tanned a deep brown. His head was almost completely bald and his eyes of a startlingly clear blue.

"Ladies and gentlemen, I don't think there is any need for me to introduce Mr. Harry Shelford."

Even Steve was completely taken aback by the suddenness of the development. Only Temple, Mrs. Draper and Shelford himself were unmoved. Westeral could not have looked more discountenanced had Mephistopheles himself risen out of the ground in front of him.

"Great heavens!" exclaimed Sir Graham, backing away from Shelford as from a spectre. Vosper, balancing on the tips of his toes, hesitated and wondered which of his two suspects most deserved his attention.

Temple looked across the room to give Charlie a warning glance. For an instant nobody's eyes were on Westeral. In that split second he moved with the speed of a man who has had the fright of his life.

Two strides towards the door brought him behind Mick Tyler. By that time the automatic which had lain concealed in his jacket pocket was in his right hand. It was a small black French weapon with a wicked extension to the barrel which his father had brought back from France in 1918. He jabbed the muzzle into Mick's spine, seized her arm and dragged her roughly to her feet. He backed against the wall, shielding his own body with hers.

"If anyone makes a move or tries to stop me I shall shoot Mrs. Tyler. It's as simple as that."

Nobody there had the slightest doubt that he would carry out the threat. His voice, high-pitched and unnatural, carried a curious kind of authority. Steve could not look away from his eyes. It was as if a veil had been drawn away from them, revealing something stark, staring and terribly frightening. He was almost unrecognisable as the suave young man who had arrived late for the party.

In the silence Temple's voice sounded as loud as a Sergeant Major's roar.

"Hold it, Charlie."

In accordance with their prearranged plan Charlie had brought his automatic up to the ready as soon as Shelford made his appearance. But Vosper's manœuvres had blocked his line of fire and he had been trying vainly to get Westeral in his sights. Westeral jerked a quick glance towards him and then his eyes went on roving restlesly over the room.

"So that's it." He pushed the barrel harder into Mick's back and she winced. "Throw the gun down on the table. Hurry now!"

"Do as he says, Charlie," Temple called calmly.

The gun landed on the table with a woody clatter. The bottles and glasses jingled for an instant. Down in the car park below someone who had forgotten to turn the ignition on was taking hell out of his starter and battery.

"Remember now," Westeral warned. "If anyone tries to follow I shall shoot Mrs. Tyler."

Mick Tyler's face was yellow. The muscles round her jaw had gone flabby and her cheeks seemed to be hanging like dead flesh. She stared at Temple as if trying to convey some mute appeal. She did not try to resist Westeral as he moved along the wall, feeling for the door with one hand behind him. His hand encountered the key, removed it from the lock. He opened the door and with a quick glance reassured himself that the corridor outside was empty. He placed the key in Mick's hand.

"Put it in the lock – on the outside," he ordered.

Mick's hand was trembling so that she had difficulty in inserting the key. Westeral's eyes never stopped their restless questing. When the key was in place he gave Mick a sudden pull, slammed the door and turned the key in the lock.

"He won't get far," Vosper remarked confidently. "I have men downstairs."

Hardly had he spoken than there came the sound of a heavy fall just outside in the corridor. Temple rushed to the table and picked up the automatic that Charlie had dropped. As he did so two shots sounded in quick succession, so loud that they might have been fired in the room itself. Lucille Draper screamed and clapped her hands to her ears.

"Stand back a bit," Temple warned. He glanced at Steve. "Put your fingers in your ears."

Steve stopped her ears while he fired four shots into the wood-work round the lock. Splinters flew back and at the first tug on the handle the door came open.

Signalling the others back Temple stepped cautiously out into the corridor, with Vosper at his heels. On the floor, close to the wall, Westeral lay pinioned by Mick's heavy body. She had overthrown him, clasping his arms with hers and bearing him to the ground by sheer weight. By firing into her chest at point blank range Westeral had only sealed his own fate. Mick was slumped across him, her limp dead weight imprisoning him, her arms locked behind his back.

He saw Temple's automatic aimed mercilessly at the centre of his brow, and lay back.

"Throw your gun clear."

Westeral had to struggle to free his arm and send the gun sliding across the floor. Temple kept him covered while Sir Graham and Vosper gently lifted Mick off him and laid her on her back.

"Mrs. Draper," Sir Graham said over his shoulder. "Please go and telephone for an ambulance at once. Shelford, go to the head of the stairs and prevent anyone coming up to this floor."

As Westeral scrambled to his feet Vosper whipped a pair of handcuffs from his pocket and clapped them on his wrists. His jacket and shirt front were already stained with Mick's blood.

"I advise you to keep very quiet now, my lad," Vosper said in a dangerously gentle voice.

Mrs. Draper and Shelford had moved away to execute Sir Graham's orders. Mariano and Davis were standing in the doorway staring down at the prostrate Mick. Steve dropped on her knees beside her and pillowed her head with one hand. She opened her eyes and a spasm of pain crossed her face. She stared at Steve and then shifted her gaze to Westeral.

"You chose the wrong person," she whispered. "Betty's mother."

CHAPTER TWELVE

That evening Sir Graham and Vosper came for drinks to the flat in Eaton Square. The occasion took the form of a celebration, for the doctors who had operated on Mick Tyler to remove the bullets had declared that she was out of danger.

"What will you drink, Sir Graham?" Steve inquired. "Sherry or a cocktail?"

Sir Graham glanced at Temple quizzically and then laughed.

"Sherry please, Steve. I think I shall be off cocktails for quite a while after this morning's experience. You know, at one time I didn't think that husband of yours was going to pull it off."

Temple spoke over his shoulder as he drew the cork from a fresh bottle of Tio Pepe.

"When Westeral told me I hadn't an atom of proof I knew he was stating the simple truth. That is why I had to build up so elaborately to Shelford's entry. My only chance was to shock him into betraying himself."

"You shocked him, all right," Vosper agreed. "You shocked a few other people as well, including me. Of course, there are still a few odd points to be cleared up, sir."

"I realise that. Are you going to have a cocktail, Inspector, or would you prefer a whisky and soda?"

"I think this calls for a whisky if I may, sir."

Temple poured the drink and handed it to Vosper.

"I couldn't cover every detail in such a short summing up, but I believe that most things click into place now that we know the main outlines. I don't suppose you'll have any difficulty in getting statements from the conspirators."

"They're ready to talk," Vosper said. "This business is certainly going to raise hell in the horse-racing world. There's never been anything like it before."

"I'm afraid the papers are going to be after you, Temple," Sir Graham said. "I shan't be able to hold out on the press much longer."

"Just give Steve and me time to get out of the country," Temple laughed and started to rattle the cocktail shaker vigorously.

"Seriously, though, Temple, you've done a wonderful job. I don't say it's always true, but this was one case which normal police methods would never have solved. The Tyler mystery would have been just another of those unexplained crimes."

"It's kind of you to say that, Sir Graham." Temple took the stopper off the shaker and poured two foaming White Ladies into his own and Steve's glass. "I'd never have brought it off if Shelford hadn't agreed to the plan I suggested to Lucille Draper on Friday morning."

"Oh, Sir Graham," Steve cut in impulsively. "I do hope they'll be lenient with him."

"He'll get off lightly," Sir Graham assured her. "As for the others, I have a shrewd suspicion we shall never hang any very serious charge on them. Though I somehow doubt if Mr. Tomlinson's entries will figure in any more race programmes."

The telephone rang abruptly and with a muttered excuse Temple crossed the room to answer it. Steve kept the conversation going while he talked, one hand held over his right ear. When he laid the receiver down and turned back to his guests he was trying to suppress a grin.

"Friend Pasterwake again," he told Steve. "He's going to be in Rome for the next three weeks as from to-morrow. He wants us both to fly out so that we can continue discussions about the film there. How does the idea appeal to you?"

"But that's marvellous, darling." Steve's eyes were shining. "I can think of nothing better than a holiday in Italy."

"Good," Temple went back to the table and took up the receiver again. "That's all right. My wife and I will meet you in Rome in say five days' time. Excelsior Hotel? Very well. Good-bye."

Sir Graham had put a hand on Steve's shoulder and was shaking his head admonishingly.

"You're making a big mistake, my dear Steve."

"Oh?" Steve looked up into Sir Graham's face. "Why do you say that?"

"Haven't you heard that the daughter of an Italian Cabinet Minister has just been kidnapped? I'm pretty sure that if your husband goes to Rome it won't be long before he gets himself mixed up in the case."

Temple said: "It's odd you should have mentioned that, Sir Graham." His brow had furrowed and he was staring into his cocktail glass. "I read the report in this morning's paper. There were several features which intrigued me—"

Steve caught Vosper's eye and suddenly burst out laughing. Temple looked at her in surprise.

"What is it, Steve?"

"By Timothy, darling," said Mrs. Temple. "Here we go again!"